A Message from Rosa

A Message from Rosa

AN AFRICAN DIASPORA NOVEL IN SHORT STORIES

Quince Duncan

Para realizar pedidos de este libro, contacte con:
Palibrio LLC
1663 Liberty Drive
Suite 200
Bloomington, IN 47403
Gratis desde EE. UU. al 877.407.5847
Gratis desde México al 01.800.288.2243
Gratis desde España al 900.866.949
Desde otro país al +1.812.671.9757
Fax: 01.812.355.1576
ventas@palibrio.com
436814

ACKNOWLEDGEMENTS

THESE stories are works of fiction, but they are all based on true stories, told by many people, over hundreds of years. Together they form the saga of the Yayah people, a novel in stories.

In the research done to write them, the following sources were of great value: my Grandfather, James Duncan, who introduced our Ashanti heritage to me as a child. Richard Hart, *Esclavos que Abolieron la Esclavitud*. Robert B. Fisher, *West African Religious Traditions*. Cheikh Anta Diop, *Civilization or Barbarism*. Martin Luther King Jr., *Stride Towards Freedom*. Joel Rufino Dos Santos, *Zumbi*. María Lourdes Siqueira, *Os Orixás*. Margaret Shinnie, *Ancient African Kingdoms*. May Opitz, Katharina Oguntoye, Dagmar Schultz, *Showing our Colors*. Miguel Barnet, *Biografía de un Cimarrón*. Susan Feldmann, *African Myths and Tales*. Nina S. de Friedemann, *La Saga del Negro*. Rhoda L Goldstein, *Black Culture and Life in the United States*. Rupert Lewis, *Marcus Garvey, Anti-Colonial Champion*. Musée du Noveau Monde, «Visitor's Guide» (France). W.O. Blake, *Slavery and the Slave Trade*. João Medina and Isabel Castro Henriques, *A Rota dos Escravos*. Théophile Obenga and Simão Soindoula, *Racines Bantu*. Mazisi Kunene, *Emperor Shaka the Great*. Nicolás Ngou-Mve, "El Cimarronaje como Forma de Expresión del Africa Bantú en la América Colonial". Nina S. de Friedemann, "Ma Ngombe en un Palenque de la Diaspora en

Colombia". Rogelio Martínez Furé, *Poesía Anónima Africana*. Ivor Morrish, *Obeah, Christ and Rastaman*. Manuel Lucena Salmoral, *Los Códigos Negros de la América Española*.

Special thanks to World Council of Churches', "Programme to Combat Racism" (Geneva); to Ruth Hamilton (In Memoriam) and her "African Diaspora" Program in Michigan, U.S.A; to Luis A. Beltrán and his "Estudios de Africanía" Program in Spain; to Luz María Martínez Montiel, former director of "Nuestra Tercera Raíz" Program in Mexico, and to Unesco's Slave Route Project.

Special thanks to my dear friend Marcy Schwartz, who took a first-hand look at the initial draft copy and to Dr. David Flory who invested many days of hard work revising the final text.

And, everlasting gratitude to my family, who supported my effort wholeheartedly.

AFROREALISM

A Declaration in honor of: Richard Jackson, our modern
Orisha of Visibility and Manuel Zapata Olivella,
the Orisha of Convocation.

Multiple voices.

Stories stemming from a common original African
ethnicity rooted in spirituality and reverence for the Ancestral
Lore, a common experience with abduction, enslavement,
colonialism, displacement and racism.

And, as our journey unfolded, stories told and retold
by an infinite number of narrators: stories recreated, never
the same, and yet always the same. Ancestral voices forever
present and always alive, in our daily lives. A thousand
readings of the same experience.

They help us to resist, to keep, to survive. And they live
on. They come back to us. They help us build the present.
Afrorealism. Fragmentary consciousness reenacted. The
building of a Universal Afro Identity. A new wholeness,
a healing process. A call for diversity. All inclusive. All
dignified. All recognized.

And from Afrorealism to the world, this drive for survival
for all of mankind, with energy, space and time for every
single expression of humanity. That is survival. Survival in
plenitude.

Dreaming

Keep vigil until the tree flourishes. Keep vigil until the dawn of better days. The Ancestors will let you know when the time has come and you will be blessed for that reason."

THERE is a strange look on her face. Or maybe it is a detail that I have not noticed before. Very strange indeed, since I have looked at that face so many times day after day. I can close my eyes and draw that face accurately, including the pores. She gets up from her seat, walks toward the window and rests her hands on the frame. Her eyes reach out for The Tree. That is what we call it: The Tree. I take my shepherd's rod and lifting myself, join her next to the window. There it is standing upright after so many years.

- My father brought it from Timbuktu. He then worked with am…oh, what is his name? Yair…am, Yaír El Soleiman …or something like that –she said.

I am aware of the story. It is one of those typical stories, told over and over again. Renovated always, passed on from mouth to mouth, each new version adding color here and there, a little more nostalgia, and sometimes a better perception of the matter.

- I believe that now a day they call them "anthropologists." No, no, that is not the word. That is not the word.

I look at her, searching for the new detail. It is essential for me to clarify what is this unexpected element that I perceive on her face. The element that I can assert is there but cannot be distinguish. I know I will have no peace until I achieve my objective.

- No, they are not anthropologists –she says, speaking to herself; pausing, as if to give place to a third thought and then adding with total conviction:
- Well, let me see. In fact they called them "wise men," men of letters.

I know this story by heart from beginning to end. Suddenly she smiles.

- My father brought me this little tree and told me to plant it. My mother could not understand why. From her point of view, it was just not appropriate. In any event, some days later I planted the tree. My father sat down on the bench watching me, his eyes shining with admiration for a daughter he loved deeply. But, mind you, I must say in his defense that even when he did show certain preference toward me, this did not stop him from being a good father and husband to all of us. He was completely faithful to his duties of rotation, giving much attention to each one of his wives. But I must acknowledge, he did show preference towards me, and this made my mother sick and had my older brother fuming with jealousy. Simply, they could not understand it. "It is as if that girl is your eldest son. You treat her like a boy and that is not right. Let her grow like a woman, like the woman she is." But my father simply ignored every word she said. He would just lift his hand, rub my head and smile. "Beautiful Mother of the World, my lovelychild, you, as if God's Feminine Persona; that tree will be the guardian of your spirit. Keep vigil until the tree flourishes. Keep vigil until the dawn of better days. The Ancestors will let you know when the time has come and you will be blessed for that reason."

But the tree never flourished. So maybe it was her father's heritage. that kept the candle burning. After all these years, she has been driving on, challenging, struggling to survive through sheer force of will and never settling down for a moment. It was not only to maintain life. It was much more than that. But neither was it life in fullness, as far as I can see. There is no fullness because she yawns daily with nostalgia, hoping to see her father's words coming true. She lives her life hoping to see if her people have kept or recovered the supreme dignity of the ancestors, the community and the traditions that give us our identity, the cradle of the ones to come. For in reality, no one is actually dead. That is, if they keep the Ancestral Spirit alive, renewing the clans of our nation. She went about wondering if they had chosen to build their homes like ours, and if they chose to return, would they be alive like people should be, or simply subsisting with a hollow mask of vitality.

- I am tired.

I had never heard those words coming from her lips before. Beyond doubt this is a very atypical day. The sun is not in its best position. The day is not dark or hot, or cold. It is lukewarm. Not a brilliant day. Not a gray day. It is just there. It is just a day.

- I think I am simply going to lie down and sleep. I have been giving it some thought for many days now, you see. It is easy: one puts one's head down like this and sleeps. That's all.

That is more than I can bear.

I can still remember the day when the Red Cross arrived in our town. There was a young boy with some type of illness unknown to us. So they went for the Red Cross. By then I was already middle aged, but I had never seen a syringe before. The doctor, or missionary or whatever he was, mercilessly sank the needle into the boy's flesh and it took two strong men to hold him. Later the boy told us that he felt the sting of twenty bees.

Now I am feeling like the boy, with the abrasive sting of twenty bees piercing into my soul. That is the sensation that her words provoke. Twenty bees, stinging directly here, close to the heart.

- You just can't – I manage to say.

- There is not much to it – she says bluntly –any one is able to. Her eyes suddenly brighten up with a touch of maliciousness.

"There is no impossible" was one of her favorite comments.

- Any way, I am tired.
- But...

"Tired." I would never have attributed such words to Aba.

- It is no time to be tired. Mind you, we have waited for many, many years. You have waited. I have been here, waiting with you. I have never left your side. I have been waiting, because you wait. So it is absolutely ridiculous that after so many years, you're simply going to toss everything into the ditch and lie down to sleep. And so you're going to let the laugh of the hyena take possession over our nation and wipe out our memories, leaving no trace of us, not even of the last of us.

She looks through the window, into the hot-humid yard. And when she speaks, it is as if it has taken her all these years, every day of them, every single minute to pronounce what seemed to be the sentence of a judge.

- There are no memories of us left. We are the last ones. Who but both of us remember the Yayahpeople? The truth is, Kwame, I believe that I have waited too long and it is now time to sleep.

Now I see the small wrinkle on her forehead. That is it. A small-single wrinkle, and yet that small detail is making a world of difference.

- You should not sleep now –I heard myself saying, appealing to that calm state of mind that only comes from years of experience. As if it was an order; as if she was prone to receiving orders.

She turns to look at the tree again, and adds...

- My father had the very best intention, but the tree never flourished.

I don't like to hear her speaking of the past as if life was over. She stands facing three hundred years of hope. I, on my part, have waited with patience. I have endured with hope, hope and hope. I have nurtured myself with stories, with legends, with the tales of ancestral dreams, with the wisdom of adults. And I have endured.

- Thank you –she says, and her voice seems to come from the very depth of her whole being.

- What? – I ask, somewhat stunned.

-Thank you - she says –before I descend into the Valley of Forgetfulness, I would like to tell you that I am grateful to you. Thank you, Kwame. You have been more than a husband to me.

Well, it is finally my turn. It's a question now of finding the right words.

- Well, Aba, if that is so, I deserve one last favor.

- No tricks…

She is smiling now. A sad soft smile, it is, but nevertheless more than I expected.

- Give me one month to find out about them.

- Ah, come on Kwame! I can not believe what I am hearing. We have been waiting for years. Who knows how many years it has been! I cannot even remember if the King of England was Henry or George. Anyway it doesn't matter. It is only that, well, we have been here, I mean, wishing to see any sign, any message that could indicate to us that the curse is over. And nothing happened. Now I am too tired to accept this fantasy of yours.

- One month – I implore –One month!

She sighs. And I can again see the small wrinkle on her forehead and the strange-sad smile. Another birthday. In one month anothercomplete year and the story will come to an end. For better or for worst.

- The tree will flourish, I promise.

- How can you promise such a thing, Kwame?

The Elder, her grand-uncle, the foundation of the family, loved them dearly and was very proud of his children and nephews. He had been enslaved and sold when he was a boy, for reasons that he never quite understood. He was traded to an Arab, a man of letters, and with him he had the opportunity to travel to Timbuktu. There he learned how to read and write, gradually becoming the right hand of his master, who indeed was more than a father to him.

And so after thirty years he recovered his freedom, which he managed to buy with hard work and loyalty. His master was leaving, heading north, and so the future Elder returned to the south, and prepared to claim his place among the Yayah, his people.

Fortunately for him, he had kept in his memory the details of his lineage. He could proclaim it to the town in the presence of his clan's Guardian of Tradition. The people celebrated the return of this hero "who had gone from us and now has returned to us", and they gave praise to the ancestors that looked after him and brought him back.

The Elder set out to take his place among the Yayah people, ascending through the rites of initiation without setbacks. His Aunt Akua nominated him among all her nephews to become the next King. When he became the ruler, to the bewilderment of many old men, he reformed the laws and the traditions. This made them to burst in anger. But time and again he bribed them into "civilization" as he termed it, by choosing sons of each one of the main families and sending them off to Timbuktu, to become learned men, to become expert interpreters of the law.

But he also respected the bulk of tradition, avoiding religious discrimination among the Yayah people. On the contrary, in conformity with the ordinances of the Ancestors, all groups were represented in his court. So he took guards from each clan, from each religious group, and he married women from different families, always maintaining a perfect ethnic balance.

Aba's father had twelve sons and daughters when the King sent him as head of the escort that led to Timbuktu; the last Yayahs that ever had that opportunity. She did not remember the departure, but she has never forgotten the return.

It was a sunny day. The inhabitants of the town and the King congregated in the square in order to receive the travelers as they came back after leaving the last five Yayah students in Timbuktu. The return of Yayah travelers to the town was always an important event, because of the fascinating stories they told about their trip.

She was there, just another little girl holding on to her mother, tense but full of pride. After all, she was the daughter of the head of the escort, a man of whom all spoke well in the town. He was a direct descendant of the Elder, "Our King", the old men of the town said. "The wisest man ever, the receiver of the ancestral wisdom, the controller of the power of the two worlds."

She will indeed never ever forget when her father, after paying his respectful visit to his uncle the King, finally made his way home, greeting his wives, and celebrating as if he was out of his mind until he took notice of Aba.

- Is she… is this the girl that made my life happy when I was sick?

- Yes —her stepmother said grudgingly - The same girl. Your first wife's eldest daughter. But here is my boy - she said —your son. He is the first male. He came from my womb. And I am your favorite.

Aba's father ignored the unexpected provocation, came directly to her and gave her a small plant. Its roots were wrapped up neatly in leaf. He smiled at her and said, "let's plant it." And the invitation hurt her stepmother and stirred sweet revenge in the heart of Aba's mother, although on the surface she acted disapprovingly. But again, Aba's father ignored them. After all, he was the son of a man who changed the Yayah people forever.

A week later she planted the tree. Her father told her that from that moment onward it would be a symbol of the ntoro, the vitality of his family. And from then on the tree and Aba have been relatives. But she gave fruit, the tree never did. She has been mother to eighteen children, some of which she had lived to see dying. But her concern was for those about whom she knew nothing. Sixteen of them unaccounted for. Some said that Aba's stepmother cursed the tree, but she always denied it. The explanation was simple —it had not given fruit because better days were still ahead.

However, in the latter part of her life, she had begun to consider and talk about the curse, in an ambiguous way.

Aba was only eight years old when her father brought the tree from Timbuktu and told her to plant it. Now space and time seem to mix. Time seems to have stopped in our town. Space here has been untouched except for the lights coming from our kerosene lamps and those immense man-built "iron birds" that from time to time fly noisily over the region. But, yes, although it is painful to admit it, the beauty of life has left us.

- We have endured far beyond our time. We have endured to see this terrible and never-ending war, waged on us without compassion. For never before in the history of mankind has there been a war so cruel, so ruthless, and so senseless. In all these years, there has never been a single moment of peace. Not a single day without some sort of action, some sort of blow, inflicted as a reminder of our subordination, of our captivity. Our pride does not allow us to admit it. But our kings are bush kings. They are kings in hiding. Our history, no matter how glorious, has not been registered in books and the vigor of our drums and the clear sound of our poets thrive on the border of death. We are an invisible people. So, do not bother me any more —it is a time to rest. It is time to close the open cycle.

- But Aba, if a beast has been roving about our house, it is dangerous to fall asleep with an open door. So let me try to lay down this burden before sleeping.

- All right -she says, and this time seemingly, tears came to her eyes –I won't destroy your last hope.

The Battle

On the left, detail of a wooden sculptor by Mario Parra.
Honoring Dr. Duncan.

I closed my eyes for a moment. I closed them to postulate her survival. She would live on. No matter what. There she would be, there she will be until the circle closes and her children come back home to her.

AS far as I remember, for many years we had been at war with the Fulahghi. In my great-grandfather's days, there was peace in the region. But, as we later discovered, a not very common people, with very white skin and blue eyes, had arrived at what I found out later was "the coast."

Both the coast and the newcomers had been just part of our legends. While there were stories told about them, they were never taken seriously. We knew about White people. According to our storytellers, in the old days they had come to trade with us. But that was legend, only stories told to put us children to sleep.

But we were painfully finding out that those stories were more than myths. The Whites came from a very distant land, which I encountered later in a very hurtful way. These blue-eyed White people were searching for slaves relentlessly. As I understood the matter, they had conquered a very big island, very different from theirs. A serpent-like island, it seemed, uncoiling. According to the information available to us, they had practically killed all the native inhabitants of the island, so they came to our region, capturing people to restore the population they had wiped out.

Seemingly, they wanted to create a new race in the island. A docile race, willing to work for them. Boys of dark skin that would bear on their shoulders the life of White boys.

So it was at the beginning.

They were willing to buy all the enslaved people available. But when there were no enslaved people around they offered to buy free men. And that was how they got the nations of my region to engage in big wars –a region that I have come to understand is called Africa. These wars were waged to capture free people, enslave and sell them to the outsiders.

As I remember, my grandfather himself was a slave owner. According to the tradition of my family, the first people enslaved by us were captured in war, after our town successfully resisted an attack. Those captured were allowed to live in exchange for their service. My grandfather's slave accepted the deal on the condition that he could keep his own slaves. They had also been captured in battle.

So there were three enslaved people at home. But slavery in my town was very different from what I have seen in these lands. An enslaved person was an unpaid servant. He didn't work more than the rest of us. We did not allow him to eat with the free because only those who share our common soulcan rightfully eat together and of course they should not engage in any sexual contact with our young people. But we didn't practice wild whipping or mutilations. We didn't mark them with hot iron. There was no raping of the women, and by the second generation they had already become part of our community.

That morning when the Fulahghi band attacked our town, we were all at home, preparing breakfast, while we enjoyed the brilliant morning sunshine. For more than five years, we had succeeded inkeeping this terrible band aloof. It was a great achievement, considering that the band was integrated by about twenty thousand men, most of them Fulahghi. But many of them were former enslaved people liberated from captivity. As a general rule, they had no idea where in the world they were, so they preferred to become part of the band.

Unfortunately, that morning, the guards fell asleep. The warning drums were not heard until it was already too late. Our men reacted with courage. They took their weapons and ran toward the gates of the village. Our women matched them, brandishing swords and chanting war songs.

And mind you, that is life. For five years we had resisted successfully. We had survived. Faithful observers of the teachings of our ancestors, our town went to the fields with their weapons. We kept control over our territory. No slave trade was allowed in our land. As I said before, the only enslaved people permitted were the prisoners of war, whose lives we spared in exchange for their labor.

But that morning our clan lost many of its most brilliant sons and daughters in combat. They went down doing their very best to protect our freedom. For so many years and now, unexpectedly, death came creeping over us, taking advantage of the negligence of those who had otherwise been loyally vigilant.

For when our warriors were finally able to come to grips with the events, take their weapons and get to their positions, the enemy had profited from our errors, surrounding the village. In spite of the courage of our people, it had become almost impossible to defend the five or six square kilometers of the town.

Our people, about twelve thousand in total, fought fiercely, defending our territory with dignity. It was a matter of survival – we all knew it. Even the children, knew it. And indeed after about three hours of fighting, they broke our barrier and penetrated our lines.

My father came rushing to our house and told us that we should disperse into the forest. One of my aunts had died, he said, fighting courageously. My mother took a few things from the house and with my younger brother in her arms, crying, my sister on her back and myself running desperately behind her, we plunged into the forests. It was a terrible thing trying to make our way through the bushes. I mean, with the bramble and especially the thorns. The men had sowed them as an additional defense and they had been a blessing to us. But in our moment of flight the thorns became a curse. We could not cross the field. Our feet were bleeding badly by the time the bandits caught us.

A wild looking individual captured my mother and my siblings. They put ropes around Mama's throat and bound her to some other captive woman. Another bandit, obviously a ruffian, captured me in spite of my bold effort to get away and to free my family. Mother screamed and cried in vain. She wanted them to at least keep us together. But there was no possible way to communicate, no consideration whatsoever, no place for human feelings.

Death had made its way into our village. Plenitude was over. As they led me out of the town, along with my family, I saw grandmother Aba at the edge of the forest, hidden behind a tree that she loved dearly. I was not close enough to see her crying, but I could sense the tears. I looked away in another direction. On the one hand I could not accept her helplessness, and on the other, it was that natural instinct of mutual protection engraved in our hearts. Maybe grandmother would survive.

I closed my eyes for a moment. I closed them to postulate her survival. She would live on. No matter what. There she would be, there she will be until the circle closes and her children come back home to her.

I was unexpectedly hit on the back. It was like the sting of a hundred wasps. Yes, wasps, the first lash of captivity. I opened my eyes as wide as I could, holding my breath as if to stop the pain. I felt a bucket-full of tears choking me. But I didn't cry. I just looked at the enormous Fulahghi that now considered himself my master, trying to gather strength from the ancestors, from our beloved king, from Kwame and Aba my grandparents, from my loving mother and from my uncle who brought to our families the light of Timbuktu. I could not match the huge Fulahghi's force, so I did what I was supposed to do –despise him.

This I did with a solemn and manly pride. I laughed at him boldly and I spat in his ugly face, and prepared myself to block the tears when the whip ripped into my skin.

LAST DEFENSE

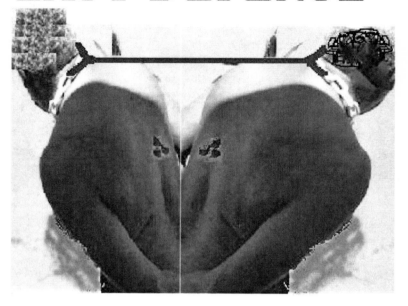

Quickly –and rather skillfully –his hands were tied together, in spite of his courageous resistance, and it took three men to get the yoke around his neck and to couple him up with another captive. Even then he tried to continue resisting.

HOW can the story be told properly?

After telling his wife to take the family and hide in the bushes, the warrior headed back to the battlefield. He ran briskly, rather desperately by his father's house. He had almost passed by when he became aware that a Fulahghi column had managed to penetrate into the village, and apparently had been attacked and eliminated by the old people who made up the last defense. His heart sank when he suddenly saw a Fulahghi heading toward his father's door.

Caught for a moment between his responsibility to return to his post and the inner call to defend his own, the warrior hesitated long enough to see the invader bend over, shout and fall on his face, bleeding out of his chest that had been torn by a spear. It took a blink of the eye to see the shadow-like figure recovering the weapon and then disappearing into the safety of the trees. He felt his family pride growing again and recognized the eyes of his father, smiling as he defended life.

Such was the irony of the human condition, to live and to die, to give birth and to kill, on the never-ending road to survival.

His mother's face came before him for the last time. She was standing under her favorite tree, the same old tree, with its myriadlegends. A gift from her father it was, and she had planted it, uprooting traditions, making new. He felt such deep love, and with that he ran briskly on to battle.

It was evening already, although the sun was just halfway on its daily journey. It was evening already, in spite of his father's brave deed. Because it took a whole lot of pluck at his age to eliminate one of those Fulahghi savages, with such an able use of the spear. It was evening already, even though it appeared otherwise.

He plunged into the battle, only to be ambushed and reduced to captivity.As he made his last effort to inflict harm on his enemies, he felt the very first blow of humiliation. Quickly –and rather skillfully –his hands were tied together, in spite of his courageous resistance, and it took three men to get the yoke around his neck and to couple him up with another captive. Even then he tried to continue resisting. But the other man's voice made him halt.

- You're going to break your neck and choke me –the voice said, and it was only then that he lifted his eyes to look at the scene.

It was over. It was evening already. Ahead, he could see a woman from his village, keeping pace with her young child wrapped in a colorful cloth tied firmly to her waist. Beside her, her young son, wailing, his hands also tied together, moving as if by an invisible hand, moving on. Further ahead, he saw two brave soldiers from his village, coupled together. The first had his hands tied together in front of him, while the second man's hands were bound behind him. The men were yoked together at the neck. The road, the whitish road, the dust, as far as the sweat in his eyes allowed him to see, a formidable column, two men, women and children, then two men, women and children, then two men…

"Damn beasts" he manage to whisper as they went by the boabob tree. He tried hard to take a good look at his captors. He wanted to remember them. He intended to keep the bitter memory as long as possible. Maybe the survivors from his village would rescue him. Maybe his family could pay ransom. He had heard stories about a pale race on the coast. As far as he knew, they bought enslaved people, but at the same time craved gold. So, maybe…Or even before. If his village could get organized on time, maybe they could keep in touch and come to some agreement with the horrible Fulahghi before reaching the coastline, which according to tradition was many, many days' walk ahead.

"Damn beasts" he managed to whisper as they passed the Sacred Rock where the guardian angels, known as the "tete abosoms" live. It marked the limits of his people's territory. His neck was already bruised as he and his partner marched on in an uncoordinated way with the sun biting into his flesh, harassed by those "damn beasts." Force on the way: the power of spears, of arrows, of swords. Force and power on that dusty road.

- Damn savage beasts –he burst out loudly.
- Shut up –a voice came from nowhere and bit into his back.
–Shut up and keep moving.

Night came, and captors and captives halted a short distance from the river. First there were the flies and later the mosquitoes. At night ropes around the necks replaced the yokes. The bruises, the abrasion of the neck. The stench. The unbearable stench as the men had to relieve wherever they were. The nausea. The revulsion of food being consumed in the presence of filth. Tasteless food. What happened to the yams? Bitter food. Not the healthy taste of mom's pot. No more of the sweet smell of palm oil. But above all, the anger. The humiliation of having to bear the words of the now-vanquished king: "we are a free people. We have never been and never will be enslaved. It is the responsibility of every man to fight until there is no more Yayah blood left in his body. It is the obligation of every woman to defend the village and the children, to save them from the humiliation of slavery."

So where is the King now? Where are the elders? Where are the ancestors? Will we all be forced to gather around the Tree of Forgetfulness? Will no one parade around the Tree of Remembrance in our name? Will we forever have to listen to the savage clatter of the Fulahghi so foolishly calling themselves the people? A clan-less people, that is. A wicked and godless people they are. May their gourds be always empty. May they be furnished abundantly with palm nuts from the market of the dead. May they die together and rest forever in the Valley of Death. May they never find the road back to the land of the living.

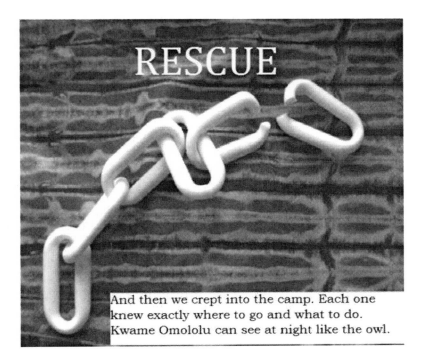

RESCUE

And then we crept into the camp. Each one knew exactly where to go and what to do. Kwame Omololu can see at night like the owl.

NOW let me see if we can get this straight. After telling his wife to take the family and hide in the bush, the brave Yayah headed back to the battlefield. He ran briskly. He had already passed by his father's house when he became aware that a Fulahghi column had managed to penetrate into the village, and had been attacked and eliminated by the old people who made up the last defense. His heart sunk when he suddenly saw a Fulahghi heading toward his father's door.

Caught for a moment between his responsibility to return and hold his ground, and the inner call to defend his own, he hesitated long enough to see his father fall and the invader's sword raising for a moment and then beginning its downward plunge, as if heralding death. He shouted but it was too late.

At that moment, literally from nowhere, a spear made its way into the Fulahghi's chest. He saw him bend over, shout and fall on his face, convulsing.

He did not see the executioner, but he could hear her laughing. It was the same voice that, at birth, greeted him to life, shouting. The very same voice that playfully used to say "Got ya" was now whispering triumphantly "Got him"; the same voice that hushed him to sleep, yes, the very same voice that just a few days ago told him with pride "you are truly your father's son. You make me live."

His father was on his feet in no time, making sure it was the Fulahghi's last day. He felt the family pride again. His mother defended life. To give birth and to kill, such is the never-ending road to survival.

"When I finally made it to the edge of the village, I came across the King's eldest son and a group of men.

- Stop" he said.
- They have got my sister" –I told him –I can't let them go.
- We'll go after them –he said –in due time.
- The time is now –I shouted in desperation –they took my sister.
- Wah key– he said and I hated him for that.
- No, it's not all right. I've got to stop them"
- Get yourself together –he ordered -you are the son of an elder. We will outwit them. In no time we will be jamming. Wah key?"

All I could do was to sit down and hit the ground with my fist. Any way, I could not rescue my sister on my own.

Late afternoon we began pursuit. Kwame Omololu was like the owl, he could see at night. The moon was in our favor. I frankly was scared. Scared by the laughing of the hyenas. I could sense the savage look of the wild cats, and tremble at the roar of the lions. I could feel deep in my heart the powerful beat of a hundred elephants in stampede. We kept our pace all night. And at dawn we watched them prepare breakfast. We watched them continue their way, our people in bondage. We saw them cross the river, the children caught in panic, the women scared to death, the men humiliated, helplessly bruised by the sticks and ropes around their throats and necks. We watch them facing the violent sun of midday, the dust at sunset. We saw them camping while It rained for a short time, and then leaving the children trembling in the cold air of night.

And then we crept into the camp. Each one knew exactly where to go and what to do. Kwame Omololu can see at night like the owl.

At dawn we cut the ropes quietly, then we send the Fulahghi guards off to sleep and we pray they would never find their way back to the land of the living. When morning came, the battle ended.

Among those liberated were about fifty Sumani people whom we brought to our village. The King had them line up in front of his house, and explained to them that they were to be enslaved. It was our right. We had captured them in battle. The women gave them food and drink, and palm oil to rub on their wounded bodies. The king made it clear to them that they were his slaves, but would be placed in the hands of some of the most important families. They should be faithful to their overseers. They also had the obligation to defend the village, should the Fulahghi or any other bandits attack us again. He also told them that they could not eat at our tables, and should not engage in any intimate relations with our sons and daughters, unless they had explicit permission from the King himself. He then hand-picked five of them to serve in his household and divided the others among the forty valiant villagers who had rescued our people.

My family was lucky; our slave had a slave of his own. So we got two. I introduced them to my wife and children, and promised them that if they worked hard and fought bravely in our battles, I would intercede with the King to make them free. Then they could continue to live with us if they chose to, or return to their village. The Sumani said he was a rich man, and that he was prepared to pay a sack of cawri shells for his freedom, if only I would let his slave go to his village to fetch his treasures. I smiled. We were just not ready for another battle.

My sister came to see me. She was crying. The danger of losing each other had made us aware of the true depth of family love.

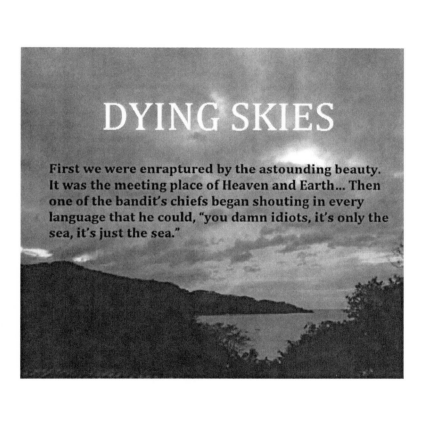

DYING SKIES

First we were enraptured by the astounding beauty. It was the meeting place of Heaven and Earth... Then one of the bandit's chiefs began shouting in every language that he could, "you damn idiots, it's only the sea, it's just the sea."

THAT night we heard some very unusual roars, like bellows, coming from the deep. And as we listened in awe, we were violently assaulted by the wind. The Fulahghi seemed restless.

At morning we were lined up very early. The routine of every day was gone. They urged us on, using whips and savage gestures, as if there was some sort of danger. We hoped. We thought we heard the cry of battle, as our people came to rescue us.

Then suddenly we came out of the bush and were astonished to see what we could not have imagined. First we were enraptured by the astounding beauty. It was the meeting place of Heaven and Earth. The dizzying rays of the morning sun, in colors, reached what seemed to be water, an absolute abundance of water! And the roar, the light but imposing bellow that came from there, or from nowhere, or from everywhere.

I evoked the songs of the griot. Could this be what our bambara slave used to call Fugundo the secret of nothing? But I answered to myself, "no it cannot be. For this is manifest, and can be seen, and it is beautiful." In the sight of such dumbfounding wonder, the Fulahghi beasts became even more violent. They whipped us down the hill toward anguish. They forced us down the hill into panic.

Then one of the bandit's chiefs began shouting in every
language that he could, "you damn idiots, it's only the sea, it's
just the sea."

I had been told stories about the sea. How it swallowed
people. From the sea, I had been told, came the White men,
those who came to trade. My grandfather told me that during
the great days of the Kingdom of Songhai a Korei-Farma was
named. He was the minister in charge of the White minorities
that lived among us. But those days where gone now, and
here we were, with no place to remember great Timbuktu,
with no place to hail the enchantment of Djenne.

They forced us into panic, as the cry went out among the
women that White men ate children. We were very close to
mutiny and after two attempts to escape, we were rounded
up and ropes were put around the necks of the mothers
permanently for the first time.

And as we came out into the open and were forced into
what they call the "square", some of the men began to curse
the Fulahghi. Others begged the Ancestors that they be wiped
out from the face of the Earth, and that there be no memories
of them in the years ahead. We prayed that their descendants
would be sterile. Others prayed fervently, "May Allah curse
them. May they be cast into eternal death."

The "square" was a large patio with thatch huts. They
were not round as they should be, but square and I guess that
was the origin of the name. The whole place was surrounded
by high walls, made of excellent timber, and permanently
guarded on every side by the Fulahghi bandits. A small stream
ran through the Square.

We were organized into small groups, each with his or
her own overseer or owner, and, band by band, taken to the
water, untied, washed and the men shaved. We were then
given an unusual serving of food, with meat, and later chew
sticks to cleanse our teeth.

Our hands were tied behind our backs, and women rubbed our bodies with palm oil. Finally, we were told to "rest."

So we went gradually from awe to anguish, then to panic, and finally terror overcame our souls, when the overseers took the first group of captives out of the camp. Those were the "king's slaves", and I was among them. But, as I was soon to discover, the name did not apply. For the people enslaved to the king in my country were privileged men. They were the defenders of the princes. They were so dignified that they had representatives in the Council that elected the Damel, our king. And they sat with full powers, as one of the four parties. I was among the enslaved of this so called "king." And as I was ushered toward the sea, I saw him for the first time. The "king" was a rather young man, not very tall. In fact, the enslaved men were evidently stronger and manlier than the Fulahghi bandits, and their king was the least among them. Although he wore a luxurious cloth over his back, tied elegantly on his chest, and had a band around his head, there was nothing royal about him.

He inspected us as if we were animals, and satisfied, lead the way. Twenty-six of us followed him —fifteen men, five children and six women. The men, coupled at the neck, were forced to walk briskly behind the "king."

As we came to the beach the gang stopped us. The "king" and his guards made way toward…

So that was it!

We advanced slowly now, while the "king" conversed with the White man. This White man was all covered with clothes. I guess it was the sun. Maybe he came from a very cold land. His whole body, except his face, was covered. He wore a hat, closed sandals on his feet, and his hands were also covered. He stood surrounded by his own guards who were also white-skinned, but wore less clothing. To the right of the leading White man, there was an odd collection of artifacts, including iron bars, bronze bars, glass, mirrors and many other items, some of which I had never seen before.

The "king" and the White leader argued for a while, and two by two, we were moved over behind him. One of the White men, who we later learned was the medicine man, examined us meticulously -teeth, arms, eyes, and to our shame and disgrace, they did not even respect the women's breast and genitals. One of the captives was not accepted, because he had some sort of sickness called "yaws", which I had never heard of before. The "king" mounted in rage and ordered him to be executed immediately.

After examination, they again bonded our hands, this time with iron cuffs. And we finally faced the sea. At some distance, the White men's vessel could be seen, a very large boat with sticks pointing to the skies, just like it was depicted on the paintings from the Kingdom of Mali.

Later we were forced around the Tree of Forgetfulnessand then into the boats; forced to become the outcast, the helpless, the useless, meat for the White men.

And they will eat my liver, these White pagans; I know they will, trying to capture the essence of my being, hoping to thrive on the strength of my heritage. Allah, what an all- encompassing feeling of terror, grinding my bones! May the Ancestors come to my aid. I will not be a slave! "Before I be a slave I'll be buried in my grave." And in this way I will come home to the Father in Heaven. I will be in his glory.

So I jumped out of the boat into the warm waters of the sea.

- Don't do that –a man shouted to me in my language, but it was too late. The sea was soft, welcoming, as a natural caress. I heard the shouts of the guards as I jumped overboard. My lungs readily took in the salted water, and I opened my eyes to see for the last time the bright sweetness of life. I saw the figure of one of the guards, trying to reach me, but I was already way down, far out of his reach. And I went down, down to freedom, down, down, down into the bliss of Allah.

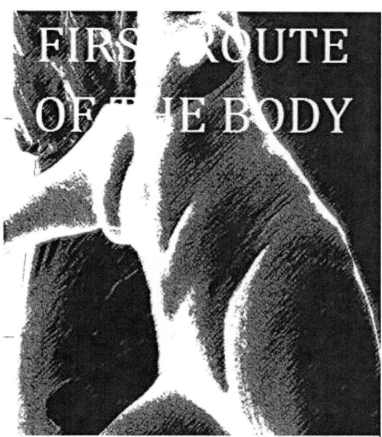

FIRST ROUTE OF THE BODY

And she felt the agony of bondage, the force of putrefaction in that body that was hers, theirs. For their bodies had become the body defiled.

IT should have been dawn. It should have been brighter. But the cabin was dark and very cold. She just could not get over her confusion. Although the cabin was dismal and chilly she could see the huge body, close to hers. She extended both hands in an effort to push it away. But it was not that near. So she held her breath to avoid the repugnant smell of bad breath coming from the body's mouth. Its eyes were red. Tears emerged copiously, and as it submitted to the laws of gravity, it mixed with the strange fluid dripping out of the body's nostrils. For the first time in her life she discovered the odor of earwax.

The body came closer. Now she could touch it, but she didn't dare. It had become too repulsive. She wanted to move her own body out of the way, but there was no response, except for the paralyzing effect of horror. Bodies sweat. Bodies produce gas. Bodies belch. Bodies expel the remnants of drink and food; and bodies like her own continue the monthly cycle of life.

The warm liquid on her naked legs soon became a nasty sticky nuisance, as it decomposed in the cold of the morning. She was there, close to the other women, seeking from their bodies the warmth she tried to give, sharing life even with those who had chosen death, refusing both food and medicine. Like the girl from the Gabon region who announced to all that "soon we shall be no more in the land of the living." A few days after she was brought on board, she began to loose weight, and refused both food and water. They whipped her to make her eat, but she kept her teeth together even unto death.

And now there was this other huge body. She got up as if to look toward the men's quarters. She could remember the stench that always came violently from between the decks, where men tried to breathe. If only they would open the hatches early today.

Memories flowing like an inner force building up. The nice warm afternoons, when we gathered beside the stream to wash our clothing and ourselves, seemed now long gone. All the women clad in a simple dress that hung elegantly from our waists. There to gossip. There to fill our jars with water, chatting, leaning on each other. There together, to help each other lift the jars from ground to shoulders. And above all the songs, the slow chanting that came from the very depth of our bosoms, and made its way over the air into the vast territory, as a reminder to all that we were the rightful inhabitants of that land and a happy people.

The body was not lying on its right side, as it should be to protect the heart. It was not packed as usual, the taller with the taller, selected for the widest section of the vessel, the shorter with the shorter near the bow. The body was suspended over her, with all the sweat and the filth, with the stench that made people sick.

Could it be one of the constables planning rape? No, he wouldn't dare. He knew that if he did that to any of the sisters, that would be the end of his life. It could not be any of the enslaved men, because although they did not have their manacles on, these had been replaced by leg-irons, so they were fastened to the ground in pairs. No, this body was not the body of any of the enslaved Africans, nor of the constables. Nor was it the body of any of our captors, for none of them would come to the "hole" or to the cabins at night.

But memories persisted, the memories of cotton and spinning wheels. The men working leather, making weapons from iron bars. Her mother and father crouched in the yard at sunset reading the Koran. And her brother, talking about his plans to travel to Mecca some day, to follow the path of Mansa Musa; dreaming that some day he would be a poet and an architect like Es-Saheli, and even may be able to see Andalusia. Dreaming about the glories of the past, hoping that the statesmanship of Askia Mohammed would surge again, and that his people would once again be powerful as they were before El Mansur sent Judar, the Spanish commander, across the desert with his four thousand Christians.

Her people fought bravely and El Mansur's mercenary army was reduced to less than five hundred at the end of the war. But swords, spears and bows were to no avail against gunpowder and firearms.

Her brother used to dream those dreams, a mixture of nostalgia and hope. The past and the future blended together in his head, dimming the present. He hated the Moroccans while despising the Fulahghi who were then not considered a serious threat.

But now, the body, coming closer. Closer. No, not closer. Becoming one. She was becoming one with the body! This body with its Yayah odor. But, was it really Yayah odor? It was becoming Yayah stench. Although it was not exactly Yayah stench, but rather Sumani stench. No, not Sumani, not Yayah, but a Yayahsumani stench. She could not remove herself from the body. She could not stand the stench. It had become too repulsive. And she felt the agony of bondage, the force of putrefaction in that body that was hers, theirs. For their bodies had become the body defiled. Bodies sweat. Bodies produce deadly fumes. Bodies burp.

All day life went on as usual. It was a sunny day, and they kept us on the deck for a long time. The women on one side of the deck, sitting or stooping beside each other; the men, shackled together in pairs. At mid-morning, meals were served, consisting of the usual pint of rice, and half a pint of water. There was an intense calm on the ship, and it seemed to advance at a very slow pace. In the afternoon we were served yams and horse-beans, and another half-pint of water.

After the last meal I was stooping carelessly when I felt that there was someone staring at me. Out of curiosity I turned around gradually, only to find myself staring back at the Captain. He looked at me in a rather rude way, which made me wonder if it was true that we were destined to be food. Or could it be sex? I could not help my self –the picture of that body came to me again, sadly! What a hard thing it is to be in the agony of bondage, not being able to get rid of the force of foulness in that body that was theirs, ours. For their bodies had become the body, our body; diluted to such degree that we may never recover.

He raised his eyes to look at the sea. I looked back at my newly acquired "sisters", some of them believers, others pagan, many high cultured women, some of high rank, princesses and slaves, old and young, all together, with no respect. At least they kept the children on deck. They would die in the hole. The cabins were no place for little girls.

No, I will not submit. I will not become the body. Never.

Late afternoon the guards began the daily routine, to have us eat yams and drink water. Then we were forced to do exercise, that is, to "jump", or "dance" as the captors called it. Those who refused to do so were flagged on their feet until they jumped. Sometimes the Captain also required them to sing.

There was this one sister from a very distant land. She was so dignified. She painted crosses on the floor every time we were brought to the deck, and whispered prayers to Jesus. According to her, she was the wife of a rich Ethiopian merchant. He got into some sort of dispute with the Beri Beri people, who in revenge assaulted his caravan and sold her as slave. Exactly how she had come so far was not very clear, but she was on the ship when the rest of us were taken on board. She said she was a member of some sort of "hurch." I think that was the word. A member of the "Coptic hurch" I think she said. I hoped that some day she would receive the True Word, and come into the flock of Mohammed.

She would start to sing on her own. She said they were songs of hope, yet I had never heard such rich melancholy coming from the voice of a woman. But that day we could not make her sing. She too could feel the vicious calm on the ship. The wind was dead, and as I said, the ship seemed to advance at an extremely slow pace.

After the singing and the dancing, the guards began hustling the women back to the cabins, and the men to the hole. But surprisingly, two guards singled me out, and led me on a very unusual route. Before I could understand what was happening I found myself being forced into what I soon discovered was the Captain's cabin. The two guards held me by the hands and feet on the bunk while a white medicine man searched my vagina without scruples. As I kicked and bit and screamed calling on the Holy Name, the medicine man's kit fell on the ground. When they turned me over on my belly to paw between my buttocks, I saw a little knife, and I knew that that would be my defense. It was placed there by the power of Allah. No doubt about that. So I calmed myself as much as I could, and let them do what they wanted to.

I had not been aware of the Captain's presence until I heard him shout. The other men backed away. So I let myself fall on the ground, to hide the knife. The guards picked me up diligently and threw me on the bed. The Captain told them to leave, but one of the guards did not obey, indiscreetly staying behind. When the Captain saw him he got into a fit of rage and threw a handspike at him. He struck him with such force on the breast that the fellow fell on his face.

The other guard and the medicine man heard some filthy expression shouted in protest as he fell, came back, and hauled him out of the cabin, leaving traces of blood all over the place.

Then the captain looked at me for the second time that day. This time I had no doubt: it was not food, it was sex. He came closer with a horrible smile on his face. My blood went cold. The whole world seemed to have come to a halt. He went to the table and poured liquor from the decanter into a cup, and drank briskly. He then poured more into the cup, and came over to have me drink. Of course, I refused. So his smile changed, and I prepared myself to receive a blow as savage as the flying handspike. But he used his bare hand this time, first his open hand and then his fist, and before I could react I felt the violence of liquor in my mouth, and in my throat. So I drank a bit to appease the captain. The smile was back on his face again.

And suddenly the grunts, the wild grunts, the bruise on my body and then in my body; the smell, a new smell, not coming from his body but from his clothes, and the odor of liquor on his breath. Bodies belch. Bodies like his own, desperately seeking pleasure; the same pleasure that he could get from striking his own guard in the heart; the same pleasure of a good meal, the same pleasure of command. Then the bellow, and the words, they must have been nasty words, and the warm liquid on my naked legs, soon to become a nasty aggravation, as it decomposed in the cold of the night.

He got up and went over for another drink. And he cleared his throat as he drank, again and again, as if he had to drink himself away from reality. He then came back and tried to repeat his "manly" deed. But by now he was very drunk, so he tried for a while and then fell asleep.

It took me some effort to release from the weight of his body. I succeeded in getting him lay on his back, snorting loudly, and bent over to get the knife.

Memories I had from long ago. It was before the Wise Men of Islam came to my people. My great-great grandmother was forced to restore the dignity of our clan. Her brother had been king far beyond the eight years that was then allotted to kings. The council had come to a decision months ago, and had told him that his reign was over. But my great great-grand uncle decided to remain in power. He had a large amount of very faithful enslaved guards that were willing to die in his defense. Since he would not give up the royal shaft, the council ordered his execution, but no one could fulfill the people's will, because of the guards. So one night, after trying in vain to convince him to just drink the tea and lie down and sleep his way off into the land of the Ancestors, my great-great grandmother took a knife. A knife, very much like the one I now have in my hand, and she cut his throat just like this, and he drowned in his blood, just like this, and she took a cloth, just like this one and dropped drops of his blood from the bed to the door, just like this, so all would believe that evidently someone managed to evade the strict vigilance of his faithful slaves.

She drank directly from the decanter, may Allah forgive her, and threw herself on the floor in the corner, and slept. The day was very much advanced when she finally awoke. She was on the deck, and they were flogging the other guard, whom they blamed for the Captain's death. More than sixty lashes. Then they rubbed pickles on his wounds. What was to be her lot? She tried hard to stand on her two legs, but fell over in dizziness. She sat for a moment, trying with all her might to recover control of herself. She begged for just one moment of soberness. She looked at her feet and her hands, and found out to her surprise that she was free. Only White men and the captive children were on deck. She was the only woman among them. Someone was supposed to guard her, but did not do much because of her state of intoxication. So this was her moment. Her only moment!

The children later told the story. She jumped to her feet, panting like a wild animal, struggling to hold her breath for a moment. The children said that it was at that very moment that someone shouted some words that sounded like "heyu de" or something of the sort and that seemed to give her strength.

She did not turn to see who the voice came from. She ran. She ran across the deck and leaped, and it was only then that they saw the rope around her neck. She leaped up into the air, the children said, and they could hear her body bouncing against the side of the vessel. The White medicine man came running after her. For a moment he bent over the side of the vessel, watching the body bounce back and forth. He took a sword from a soldier, and cut the rope, letting the body loose to disappear in the jaws of a hundred sharks.

SECOND ROUTE OF THE BODY

Yes, the same pleasure he got from a good meal. Then the bellow, and the words, it must have been dirty words, and the warm liquid on her naked legs, soon to become a nasty annoyance, as it decomposed in the cold of the night.

ALL day life went on as usual. It was a sunny day, and they kept us on the deck for a long time. There was a vicious calm on the ship, and every thing seemed to move slowly.

I was stooping carelessly when I felt that there was someone staring at me. Out of curiosity I turned around gradually, only to find myself staring back at the Captain. He looked at me in a rather rude way, which made me wonder if it is true that we were destined to be food. Or could it be sex?

He lifted his eyes and looked out over the sea. I had passed beside him when we came on board, and I knew his eyes were blue. They were as blue as the sea itself. I looked back at my newly acquired sisters, believers, pagans, some of high rank, some slaves, old and young, all together. And I knew that I could not keep myself from being caught in the force of foulness, in that body that was ours.

So these were her sisters. The term was not hers. It was used by one of the elderly women to calm a dispute. "Stop fighting each other. We should not act like enemies, we are sisters now." Among them were a very rebellious lot, indeed. They spoke a language she could not understand, and called themselves "Brong." The elder sister told her that they were "children of the keeper of the drums" and distant relatives of the Yayah people.

Late afternoon the guards began the daily routine, having them eat rice and drink water, and then getting the women back into the cabins and the men to the hole. But two guards unexpectedly singled her out, and forced her by a totally unusual route to what she then discovered was the Captain's quarters. A White medicine man came and signaled that she should lie on her back. Reluctantly she obeyed. But then there was this body, red eyes, shedding tears, the strange fluid flowing from the nostrils, the mucus and the odor of earwax.

She wanted to resist, to move her own body out of the way, but the paralyzing effect of horror kept her still. Bodies sweat. Bodies produce gas. Bodies belch. Bodies expel the remnants of drink and food.

The doctor fondled her rump, while the guards watched in delight. Then he said what she thought was "chiscleen" or something of the sort, and the captain took over. He ordered them to leave. He then went to the table and poured himself a cupful of drink from the decanter. He drank desperately, as if he had to do so, as if obeying an inner drive. Then he offered her a drink. She hesitated, since in the tradition of her family it was not proper to drink liquor. But there again were the red eyes, the tears, the fluid, the odor of earwax, the sweat, the gas, the belch, the paralyzing effect of horror. And the urge to survive, to live on in any way, because any life is better than no life. So she drank. The captain smiled.

He then pinned her down on the bunk and began the litany of grunts. That was the first time she had come that near to a Christian. The wild grunts, the bruise on her body and then in her body. The smell a new smell, not coming from his body but from his clothes. The odor of liquor on his breath. Bodies belch. Bodies, like his own, desperately seeking pleasure –the same pleasure that he could get from hanging a cabin boy who broke a glass. Yes, the same pleasure he got from a good meal. Then the bellow, and the words, it must have been dirty words, and the warm liquid on her naked legs, soon to become a nasty annoyance, as it decomposed in the cold of the night.

He got up and went over for another drink. And he cleared his throat as he drank, again and again, as if he had to drink himself away from reality. He then came back and tried to repeat his manly deed. But by now he was very drunk, so he tried for a while and then fell asleep.

It took her some effort to release herself from the weight of his body. She succeeded in getting him to lie on his back, snoring loudly. She got up, went to the table, drank directly from the decanter —may Allah forgive her —and tossed herself on the floor in the corner, and slept.

Next day she had become the Women's Overseer. She had extended both hands in an effort to push the body away. Now she had clothes to protect her body from the cold, and some extra food.

THE FIRST ROUTE TO MUTINY

Yesterday I saw birds. Birds cannot live on water alone. So we must be near land.

- I want you to translate for me.

- Well, eh...

- You told me that you speak his language.

- Yes, that's true.

- So then, will you translate or not?

- Oh, yes of course, if it's only that...

- We have to come to some agreement with them. We are ready. Yesterday I saw birds. Birds cannot live on water alone. So we must be near land. Besides, they are giving us more food. They are even trying to cure our bruises. Whatever they intend to do with us, it means that they have to do it somewhere, not at sea

- Wahkey. Let me see. Am, er... Papah, you sleeping?

- Can you?

- No, I am very restless tonight. My Chief over here wants to tell you something.

- Let him speak.

- He says, speak.

- A large number of people from our village were captured. There also around six hundred Yayahs on board... Well, I mean, there were around six hundred captives on board; men and women. And there are two elders among them. We can continue to be a people and if we wish, we can all keep together. Since we have been able to talk, not one has tried to kill himself. Yayahs are an admirable people. Our elders have given consent, and they have elected me to be the Leader. I am from the chief's family. If we return to our land, all I have to do is to report to the King, and let him decide who will rule the village. If we never get back, then wherever we may be, we will kindle the fire and survive.

- He says 'congratulations', that he wishes you the best. But that now, having heard your desires he wishes to try to get some sleep.

- Tell him I respect his desire to sleep, but that I have something else to say, and that his opinion is necessary.

- He says to speak promptly, to go to the point.

- If we could free ourselves and come to a land where we could defend ourselves, would he support us? Tell him that I know that there are many Sumani on the ship, and that although they may not be from the same village, they speak dialects of the same language, and are ruled by the same king. So if we break away, and succeed in establishing our domain on a certain territory, would they support us?

- He says you are loosing your mind. A people are a people if they have their own land; the land of their ancestors; the territory that contains their cemeteries. There is no way you can remain a people, without your Sacred Land.

- But, does he really believe that we will return to our own land?

- No. He says that the waters are too wide. We do not have vessels that could take us home. We do not know the way. We are dying. We do not have weapons, and anyway, our swords and spears cannot combat cannons. To begin with, how can you get us out of the chains? He thinks your ideas are wild.

- We have a plan. I swear by Odomankoma. Except God! By Asase Yaa, our Queen of the earth. And as you have Xango, under whose protection we will go to war. And as some of our brothers have Allah.

- The godless White man has defeated your gods. Our bodies are destined to be food, food for them and their dogs. They will eat our livers. They will consume our essence. And that way we will never be a people again. The only possible solution is to die. To lay down our bones right here at sea. Did you see the sign my brother made? The young man that jumped into the sea yesterday? He was my brother. At the very moment when he went down, he raised his hands up above the water and waved his triumph. His victory. He had set himself free. He could return to his ancestors, to our ancestors with pride. He could return to his land in spirit, and be born again. God willing.

- I understand your words, and respect your thoughts. But let me add that the tiger wait on his prey. I have a plan. We can break out of bondage as soon as land is in sight. We can make rafts; there is plenty of wood on the ship. We can make our way into the territory, and establish ourselves. We can try.

- He wishes you well.

- Help us.

- He considers it a waste of time.

- And what do you want your time for? What else can you do? You must live or die. If you give in, according to your words you will become the food of the wicked. So you will die a humiliating death. If you kill your self you may be able to return. But you may not be able to kill yourself in time. But if we fight…That's a good way to use our time.

- But then we become your servants, or the servants of the Banyoro, or of the Brongs.

- We will establish a common government. You will have a seat on the council. We will respect the Sumani people, if you can remain a people. Many of us may die in battle. But at the end, we will be a people. Not the same people that we were. We shall become a new people, mark my word, it will last, Except God.

The heat was at its highest at night. The air was scarce. Men, at night, could not breathe. They had already used too much air to exchange words. They had caused too much uneasiness trying to make themselves understood to each other, because they were so packed together that the slightest movement of one caused the uneasiness of another. So silence finally came into the hole. But many had overheard the conversation. Silence became so dense, it was almost concrete. For some reason, some of them had not become the one collective sweating body.

-I am not one of you", said a voice, breaking the silence. I am neither Sumani nor Banyoro, or Yayah, or Brong, or Yoruba. I was one of those captured by the Fulahghi when I was a young boy. Now that I am old they sell me out. I am almost dead. But if I can be of any help, count on me.

The chief smiled.

-Bless your soul, old man. Bless your soul.

Next day they saw bramble in the water. The chief sang a song to Nyame.

"Gye Nyame, Greatest God.

When the glorious morning comes your way

And the Sun shines on the stranger's sand

Heel to the rhythm of the Festival Day

All your power comes from land

Gye Nyame

Yes all our power comes from land."

And the deck joined in the chorus,

"Oh yes, oh yes!

Waiting for Festival Day

All our power comes from land

Gye Nyame."

And as they sang and jumped and beat rhythm out of the ship, the captain commented to the surgeon that the slaves were finally accepting their lot, that they were getting rid of melancholy at last.

The next night plans were explained very carefully. The drummer had had a swollen foot when he was put into chains. Now his foot was not only back to normal, but also rather lean. It was easy for him to get out of his iron legs. His leg partner will "die" tonight, and so will a few others. This will force the blacksmith to come down, along with the doctor. Then the dead will have to be taken to the deck. But since there is no space, since we are so packed together that no man can move without great effort, they will have to cut the drummer's foot lose from his dead mate. He can loosen his other foot. So he and one of the constables will take care of the White blacksmith. We need him to get rid of the iron. The man will either work or die. But if he will not work, I think once we get our own blacksmith free, we won't need the White one any more. The constable must go up among the dead. And the women will then get into such madness as to distract thecrew. And then the constable must reach the cannon, get rid of the guard and point the cannon toward the captain. But he cannot do it alone. So as soon as enough of us are free we must...

It could have been the constable himself. In fact, I think it was the constable. My father reared him with love, the very same love he showed to all of his children. The fact that he was the only son of my father's third wife did not make him special, but in no way was he degraded. He had the care and love that all of us got. In fact, he was admired as a bright young man, and every one was convinced that he was to become the most outstanding hunter in the history of the Yayah village.

Anyway, all that is now of no avail for here I am, the rope around my neck, the bruise, the sore, the sweat, the salt, the lashes on my back, one after the other, again and again, until my mind goes off in a haze, as my body looses blood, and as if it was not enough, the salt, salt on my wounds, and now this, the cannon, the cannon pointing directly at me, I could feel it, I could hear rage drumming in the hearts of our people, that we had been defeated, not because we were outwitted by the enemy, but because someone had decided that it was to his advantage to turn us in. Defeated by ourselves. We are dying.

The women screamed as they heard the explosion and saw the body disappear. They screamed as they saw the blood spilled on the deck. They screamed as they saw the head fall from the rope, and roll for a while before it came to its final halt. The women screamed all evening. And, in spite of the efforts of the constables and overseers, the women defied the night with their screams.

SECOND ROUTE TO MUTINY

In no time, about forty daring men, yelling with all the courage of their brave clans, holding on to the remembrance of their homelands, came on deck, armed with pieces of broken water-casks and wood planks found in the hole.

DAY came, and with the new day, hope. It was the day so long announced. The day of rebellion. "Kerapa" May all be well! the constable said and went up to report on the dead, as the guards opened the hatchways. The doctor came down, as expected. There was no explanation given about the death of such healthy men.

The drummer boy's mate was a strong man, although he had been suffering from melancholy for several days. But yesterday he was in good health and now he was dead. That was not unusual. What was unusual was that there were four dead men the same night. The doctor summoned the White blacksmith, because there was no way the men could get out of the hole if they did not first remove the dead bodies.

The doctor was occupied, coping with another captive who could not breathe. The blacksmith, who took great pride in his profession, had freed three men's feet and was occupied in freeing the fourth from the last dead body, when the drummer broke loose. He and one of the constables quickly took the first dead body up the stairs, with no objection on the part of the guards.

- Many dead. The Sumani king is dead –the constable shouted, as they ran to the area termed "hospital." The women were already on the deck and they heard the constable shouting "it seems like Festival Day" and it was then that the confusion began. The women screamed hysterically. A bunch of them threw themselves on the ground, convulsing and crying out with such desperation, that even the cook stopped his morning labor to look at the strange malady. The captain himself stood in amazement. But most significantly, the guard who stood by the cannon with fire ready to blast the slaves into oblivion if it was necessary for the crew's survival, was distracted long enough to lose his life. In no time, about forty daring men, yelling with all the courage of their brave clans, holding on to the remembrance of their homelands, came on deck, armed with pieces of broken water-casks and wood planks found in the hole. Moving fast they managed to disable a good number of the White hands, and they had others, even the wounded, defending themselves as well as they could with handspikes or whatever they could snatch.

The White cook managed to spill scalding water over the rebellious Africans, thus rendering some of them useless in the struggle, while a few jumped overboard. The guards, astonished, recovered in time to rescue the cannon. But from the hole came more men, five, ten, fifteen more, spreading over the deck, grabbing swords. And the women, recovering from their fit, attacked with everything available.

It seemed the desperate effort of a lost cause, since the guns succeed in cutting off the lives of the enslaved as they came out of the hole. Most of them managed to advance one or two steps, only to fall wounded or dead. Only a few managed to protect themselves, but that was all they could do. However, the struggle for the cannon continued, and suddenly a tremendous blast brought the conflict to a still.

The chief managed to stand on his feet for a moment. He saw the bodies of many of the women mutilated, among them his sister. He saw the headless bodies of White men, and the bodiless head of the Captain. The guard who had fired the cannon stood there, trying desperately to make sense out of this nonsense. Petrified as he was, he did not react when someone tossed a hatchet at him. He just stood, as long as he could, and then fell on his face, bleeding to death.

The chief saw land as he expected.

- Capture all the White men" –he ordered –and build rafts. We must make it to the shore. Take food. Take water. Take all the tools you can.

THE HALF-BREED ON HIS WAY TO HAVANA

By late morning I was on board, heading up the river. This was a good chance for me, a small Mulatto fish. I could take him up the river all right and then collect my reward. Then I could get back to shore and sell information to the Portuguese authorities. Life seemed to smile at me.

I was sound asleep in my cabin and very well at ease with my dreams when my door was kicked open violently. I reached for my pistol and knife but it was too late. Before I could actually do anything, I was reduced to impotence. Two men had my hands held tightly and a third had a knife at my neck.

- Just move, you damn worthless half-breed —one of then said to me —and I'll cut your throat.

They brought me out into the night, and as the lantern's light made me realize that I was in the presence of Orwell Boxman, I went pale. I knew I was in trouble. I owed him five slaves out of a deal that took place between us at Kamba. I had not paid him because, in the first place, I was totally convinced that he already had huge gains out of the bargain, and secondly I had moved out of Kamba and hoped never to see Boxman again. I was now caught in a debt of flesh —a slave bargain that I had not honored. I immediately jumped to my own conclusion: I could be kidnapped and sold into slavery.

- Boxman, Boxman... —disconsolately I called out his name – Boxman, let us make a deal.

- Shut up, you bastard!

It took me a little while to calm down. The men let me loose, but I was petrified, incapable of movement. I went into a frenzy-like panting, as I faced the dreaded moment when, because of my "black blood" I would be put into bondage. I had feared that moment all these years. Even when I was a successful player in the slave trade, making my living at it, I never felt secure enough. Personally, I did not consider myself a Negro. And, frankly speaking, I could not understand why, being a half-breed as I was, I was always placed in the rank of the Black people. My father was White, my mother was half White. Out of what logic should I be considered Black? In fact, my skin was light brown. In any case, since I am not White or Black, I should be considered Brown, but not Black. And that was the only thing I appreciated about Orwell Boxman, that he never called me a Negro.

- Listen carefully to me, Half-breed –he said –If you don't want to leave this world right away. Remember you don't have anywhere to go. You can't go home to your ancestors, because they won't accept the White part of your soul. And there are no Mulattos in the White man's heaven. So you better make the best of this life. You are going to hell. The devil is the only one that accepts people like you.

Orwell Boxman and his men laughed outrageously. I looked at them grudgingly, my dread turning to hate.

- There's a ship up river, eh?
- Yes, Portuguese.
- Cargo?-

Life came back to me. I could sense that his interest in me was not because of the debt of flesh. He had some sort of macabre plan going on in his White head. So I assumed the role I knew how to play very well.

- That is information. There is a price on information, you know.

-Yes, your throat.

Chills went through my body once more. Danger was not over. I had to outwit him. I had to use my African part to survive.

- Oh, well, uh... I guess there are some two hundred slaves on the boat.

- Great. Now listen carefully, Half-breed: I need a pilot. I mean someone that knows the river well. So this is your chance.

- I can do it, but you can't expect me to work for nothing.

- First I'll forget about what you owe me. Second, I'll give you a good reward if you take us up to Kakundy.

We discussed the reward. It was more than I expected, and although I did not trust Boxman, I felt happy.

By late morning I was on board, heading up the river. This was a good chance for me, a small Mulatto fish. I could take him up the river all right and then collect my reward. Then I could get back to shore and sell information to the Portuguese authorities. Life seemed to smile at me. That was normal: I was always lucky in the rainy season.

Early at night Boxman's spies came hurriedly back to meet the ship with the news. The target was just a few hundred yards ahead on the river, anchored to spend the night. We quickly manned the ship and armed ourselves with an adequate supply of guns and lanterns. Boxman did not trust me: he had kept his pistol loosely pointing at my head all day. But now, getting exited, he seemed to regain confidence.

Hidden by the darkness of the night, Boxman and his men leaped aboard the enemy's vessel like vampires attacking their prey. They yelled as they assaulted the ship, firing their arms into the air. The sleeping crew awoke to panic, and almost by instinct took refuge under the hatches, and then surrendered. I was ordered to take the helm and at dawn we aligned both vessels. One hundred and ninety slaves were transported to the other ship along with the supplies.

Boxman left the vanquished captain on a small island on the river, with six of his top men with supplies for three days.

- It will take them some time to get to civilization. The poor fellows will have to do a lot of swimming. In the meantime we will be gone.

Some of the members of the captured ship joined us. Others were left on the sail-less ship, to be rescued, make their way to the village or to the Portuguese post up the river.

I asked to be left in the village, but Boxman refused. He said he did not trust me. Anyway, he promised that as soon as we got to the river mouth, I would be paid and I would be free to leave the vessel.

Dark clouds covered the July skies, and rain pored fiercely, keeping the schooner bound to the coast alongside Cape Verde for ten days. Much to my delight, Boxman paid me, but there was no way I could get to shore. I thought the rain would submerge the vessel. The men were in a gloomy mood, because the longer they were pinned down, the greater the danger of been caught.

Boxman's fears were well founded. On the morning of the eleventh day the rain subsided. At about nine I was preparing to be taken ashore, when we spotted a "man-of-war" –an armored ship heading towards us. Boxman was extremely nervous, and he had reason to be. In many cases pirates were put to death on the spot.

- How did the news travel so fast? –he asked himself while staring at me.

We took advantage of the breeze that had sprung up after the lull and dashed away like a deer in fresh wind. The slaves were shifted as was convenient to help speed up the vessel. We tossed overboard whatever was not indispensable. The man-of-war shot at us twice and almost hit us. Boxman, out of feelings rather than out of reason or craftsmanship, ordered a light change of direction, and to everyone's delight we raged ahead faster on the new course. The Portuguese warship continued shooting at us but the cannon balls fell shorter. By noon we had advanced far beyond reach. Early afternoon, only her top-gallant was visible above the horizon.

Now, that was fine for Boxman and his men, but only partially beneficial to me. I would surely have ended up in

Brazil as a slave if the Portuguese had captured us. But what now? I had escaped them only to be carried away on an unexpected and very much undesired journey to the Antilles, where, if my luck failed, I would end up a slave, and if it didn't, I would be unable to get back to Cape Verde.

I spoke to Boxman about my lot. I was absolutely desperate. I had left some iron bars hidden under my cabin floor, a small leather bag with English pounds in the roof, and a sack of cowrieshells in a false well in the yard.

Now, on the subject of Mulattos, I had heard too many stories —the good ones and the worst ones.

- A boy like you could live like a king in Saint Domingue. You could be an official in the army if you were in Brazil — some of the voices said. But others heralded disgrace.

- Behave yourself, boy. In the West Indies you would be no more than a houseboy.

So going to The Indies was an absolute risk. Much to my luck I had a very good command of languages. For that reason, as the days went by I developed a close relationship with the crew. One of the sailors, a Spanish lad who joined us from the Portuguese ship, told me about a conspiracy on board to get rid of the Captain. One of those who joined us, a top officer, planned to kill Captain Boxman and claim the cargo. Our arrival at Saint Domingue would be the signal. He had the support of two of the five that joined us at Cape Verde and four of Boxman's own men.

I could not believe my good luck. I wrote the names of the mutineers down carefully and spoke to eight of the Black constables in the Sosso language. I told them that Captain Boxman was a good man, and that some of the "evil men" that had captured them before were on board, and planned to take over the ship and sink it —slave cargo included.

No doubt that was a very important move, to assure the support of the slaves if needed. The constables had noticed the presence of the officer, and the Captain had treated them better since he had more food and water on his vessel. So it did not take much effort to convince them.

After getting the support of the enslaved, which in a way was an investment in my own security, I spoke to the Captain. He quickly secured the arms. From the arms chest he supplied a couple of pistols to each of the loyal Whites, and a knife and a piece of cutlasses to the Blacks. Boxman very promptly seized the villains, and, tying them to the mainframe of the deck, in no time court-martialed them. He used the catto force confession from the culprits. The sentence, pronounced by Boxman himself, in the name of the jury, was very clear and was executed immediately. The ring-leader was thrown overboard with no further thought. The other men were whipped and they were held in irons until after the ship landed and the cargo of African slaves was unloaded.

The support of the constables in preventing the mutiny was favorable to the slaves. The Captain asked me to speak to them. He explained that we could not go back to their homeland, but that they would be taken to a good land and would be kept together.

Shackles were taken off during the day, and mixing was permitted among the sexes on deck. Some of the sailors, as the days went by, even shared some of their biscuits with the Black overseers. Sheets and tablecloths were torn to pieces and handed out to the women, to make their waist ties, which they were allowed to use while on deck.

I was totally amazed at the Captain's conduct, and only later did I find an explanation. He had to assure the loyalty and respect of the blacks, in order to place his illegal cargo with the least possible disruption.

The rest of the trip went by without any particular adventure, except for our encounter with nature. We were sailing in a pleasant Caribbean afternoon, near Turtle Island, when the Captain called my attention to a low bank of cloud ahead of us.

- Danger —he said.

It seemed at the moment a very foolish thing to me for us to be concerned over a whitetish cloud. The day was indeed a clear one, and all of us were on deck. We had just eaten dinner, and were taking advantage of the fresh air and the Captain's good mood, before we begin the never-ending daily ceremony of getting the slaves back into the hole and cabins.

But before I could find the right words to take the Captain's mind off what I considered a vain concern, the cloud had advanced rapidly in our direction, speeding itself over sky and water.

The Captain began shouting "A squall, a squall!" Then there was a sudden blast, like a thunderbolt, exactly over us. The mainsail of our ship burst into shreds from the bolt ropes. The deck was quickly inundated with sea water, and both slaves and crew hung on to the ship to save their lives.

The squall went as rapidly as it came, taking the lives of two Black children.

That night while sipping gin, the Captain confided to me that we were not heading for Saint Domingue any more. He had no papers, no manifest, no register, and no consignees. So he was heading to Cuba. Because of the precarious legal situation of the cargo, he had to exercise a very unusual degree of caution. That was the reason why he had worked so hard to gain certain trust on the part of the slaves. Now came the next step: to select an appropriate spot to land. It had to be a place from which he might communicate with the proper persons to place his cargo safely and profitably.

The day after the white squall our schooner was drifting with a leading breeze along the southern coast of Cuba. And as if it was a blessing from Heaven itself, we soon found a secluded cove east of Saint Iago. After landing safely, the Captain, myself and four other men made our way up to a rancho. The owner was eagerly cooperative. He rented us a spacious barn for the slaves, and his family prepared abundant meals for every one.

Once we had secured the cargo, the Captain and I mounted on well-fed horses, and, led by a guide, headed for Havana. Our guide had many questions about us. Taking advantage of my knowledge of Spanish, I answered with a lot of sweet talk, and had him spit out all the gossip about Cuba and Havana.

We were taken directly to a Spanish gentleman from Catalonia. The Captain said we could trust people from Catalonia. And he certainly did. He spoke openly to the man, asking him directly to act as consignee.

In no time, his Excellency the Captain General extended the necessary papers. The slaves were listed under names given by the officials. According to the papers, they had arrived six months before.

By the time we got back to the ranch, the slaves had been duly indoctrinated. They were all dressed up by the ranchero and his family, and had been given the necessary instructions on how to behave in their new costumes. Only a few refused to cooperate and were isolated from the others and treated harshly.

The returns were abundant. The Captain was so happy with his success that he forgave the mutineers, gave them a good amount of money and set them free in Havana. He paid me generously.

As far as the enslaved were concerned, he had kept his promise, at least to a certain extent. They were not kept together as a people, but, as was the Spanish custom, the families were sold together, or kept reasonably close, so they could have some kind of relationship, even if it were only for religious festivities.

With the money the Captain paid me I could live for a while in Havana or accept the ranchero's invitation and work with him on his farm. One of his daughters showed special interest in my strange accent and green eyes. But I knew nothing about farming. So I took advantage of my knowledge of Africa, the Portuguese pirates, and my light skin, to open my way in Havana. I was quickly employed by the Captain General himself, and settled down to grow rich and fat in Havana while dreaming my way back to Africa.

SCATARATION

- Run, Newlife, don't let them eat you. The boy fled.

NOW in the scataration, Nyamka's heart sank in sorrow. She wondered about her name and fate. Nyamka was short for Nanyamka, an Ashanti term meaning "God's gift". Where were the blessings?

Edward, the old man, looked at her anxiously. She tried to smile. Then his expression changed —now there was also sorrow in his eyes, and he looked away. It was not necessary for him to say anything. Words are not the sole conductor of thought and feelings. The spirit speaks in many ways, transcending the limits of flesh. She could not even sigh. She just sat down on the wooden bunk and silently began to cry.

A certain amount of remorse tortured her. Maybe if she had been able to maintain her integrity, if she had not panicked, if she had only been able to keep control, her son would be with her. But that afternoon, while standing in line with the little boy holding on to her, she could not bear the idea of his tender flesh being served at some White man's table. So as they both clung on to each other, she could not think clearly. It was a desperate situation indeed, and poor little Newlife would not stop crying.

Nyamka was the first wife of Nyaga and she loved him dearly. His name was well asigned by his Ashanti relatives: "Life is Precious". He was well built, strong, elegant, and above all, a loving man. They got married with much hope, and prepared to have many children. But a year went by with no sign of pregnancy. She consulted over the matter with the older women and housewives. She tried everything that they suggested. Her husband spoke to the older men of the village about the skills of love making. And he tried hard, in odd positions, at crazy hours, with all sorts of bush teas, but it was as if they had absorbed the sterility of the neighboring desert.

She became the object of gossip. That she could not bear children was a big disgrace. But when the children in the town began to make fun of her husband, and also start refusing to do errands for him, she gave in and accepted that he marry a second wife.

Sorrow crept into Nyamka's heart when, in a very short time, her rival became pregnant, and for that reason was now Nyaga's center of attention. Before the child was born, Nyamka finally became pregnant herself, turning her sorrow to joy. She recaptured part of her husband's attention, and love seemed to flow again between the two of them. Nyaga's eldest child was born seven months before Nyamka gave birth to a lovely boy, who she insisted should be called Newlife. It took a lot of effort to persuade her husband's aunt —who according to their tradition named the child. But the boy had restored her husband's loving consideration, her reputation and respect in the village. She was again the lady she had always been. No doubt her son brought new life to her marriage and boosted Nyaga's family "ntoro" the seminal root of the father. Finally they settled on Kwaku Esinam New Life. "Gold Baby, Born on Wednesday, God Heard Me and Gave New Life".

During the first months Newlife was a sickly child, but as the months went by he became stronger and brave. He resembled his father very much, and worked his little head off to imitate him in every possible way. They seemed very much like twin souls, with the same expressions, the same habits, the same funny way of facing life, as if the world were going to end and they had so many things to do before the big jam of life was over. He had no ill feelings for his brother, but it was very clear that Nyaga's second wife –whose name Nyamka chose never to pronounce, had to make a great effort to keep jealousy under control. In fact, in relation to his father's admiration, no one could compete with Newlife. There was so much affinity between the two of them that the Queen Mother once said publicly that there was no possibility of Nyaga outliving his son. If Esinam –that boy with the strange name dies, his father would go with him, leaving two widows and his eldest son behind.

On the morning in which the whole family was kidnapped, Newlife was playing at the pool when word came that White men had been seen in the area. Nyamka thought it wise to go to the pool and have the children come home. It was not safe to be out in the bush, when there were White men around. No one could prove it, but they suspected that the true explanation of the mysterious disappearance of a number of children, women and two men from the village was that they had been kidnapped by White men.

As she arrived at the pond, she saw poor Newlife struggling to free himself from his captor. Enraged, she ran toward them and with teeth, fingernails and the inner strength of a mother fighting for the life of her children, somehow, managed to free him. But as they fled they were roped by other men, and taken some way off from the river.

The most humiliating part was to see her husband and his best friend among the captives. They had also come out to fetch the children, and were ambushed. And it was painful beyond description to be separated, her husband handed over to a local chief on the way as part of the payment for the right of passage.

At least she had Newlife, yet with so many changes occurring rapidly in her life, she become very uneasy. And that afternoon, while standing in the line with poor Newlife clinging on to her feet, she had overwhelming perceptions and bereavement. Here was her son, his bravery and self confidence shattered, his body weakened by months of hardship at sea, by stale food, by lack of water, by melancholy, by longing for the warm brisk hug of his father, his twin soul. Where was her husband, the man she loved so dearly? He was the person with whom she had planed to share love, children, hopes; he was the man beside whom she had expected to grow into old age, supporting him as he gradually penetrated the inner circle of his community to take upon himself the responsibility of eldership. Where was her husband? What right had they to break up her family, to disrupt the life of her people?

She stood there in the line that afternoon, with her son clinging to her feet, well fed for the last two days, her skin shining with palm oil.

For the very first time she became aware of the situation. In the new context, all of those in line were of Black skin. There were no White captives. She stood, facing the mob of White men. They dressed oddly. And although they pretended to be listening to the man that seemed to be the leader, they were in fact staring at the people in the line.

Panic reached its peak when the leader pointed with his pistol toward the sky and fired. Then immediately the mob headed toward the line, rushing as wild a beast toward its prey. The women shouted in desperation, and many broke out of the line. It was then that she told her son to run.

- Run, Newlife, don't let them eat you. The boy fled.

Nyamka saw Edward leaving the shack. With him went all hopes of finding her son. No one in the region knew anything about a fugitive boy. For months she had lived on expectations. Edward told her that if the boy was captured by any of the slave owners he would find out soon. He had connections with the master's house slaves. The day before there were roomers about a boy someone had captured. Hope reached its peak for the last time. According to Edward, if it was Newlife, he could be claimed by the owner of their farm. Reunion seemed possible. And so that night she waited awake for Edward. In the pale light that she managed to keep burning, she could see his face.

But it was not Newlife. There was no life. No more life to live. No more love to give. No more hope to strive for. No more survival to hold on to. So after Edward left, the severe pain in her chest got worst. Nyamka managed to accommodate herself on the bunk. She could remember her husband so clearly now. She could see his face smiling at her. He was sitting beside her bed, with that very adorable smile that she cherished. Here he was, at last.

"Nyaga, she cried, where have you been? My loved one. They have not captured Kwaku Esinam New Life. He is strong like you. He will survive. He will live on. Through him we will survive. My mogya, our matrilineal heritage will not perish. It is also in his Blood. Our descendants will live in this new land. Our ancestors will be able to come back to the land of the living. Life will go on, my loving Nyaga. And maybe some day our children will find some way to make it back home, and your two sons will see the family united. Your sons are strong like you, Nyaga. Strong like you!

As she spoke, Nyamka placed her head in the lap of Nyaga. She saw the faces of loved ones smiling. And as she smiled back at them all —grandma, sister and the Queen Mother, she could perceive the sounds and orders of the village, and just before she fell asleep she saw Nyaga's second wife also smiling. "Efua" she said, Efua. And as she pronounced that name she had hated for so long, she gradually slept her chest pain away.

THE PARDA LADY

We are hard working Spanish Christian people. We are not Maroons. We don't live in the
"cumbes" and "maniles" as they call the negroes' communal ranches and shanty
townships. The Governor and the Cardinal himself can come here to see for themselves.
We pay taxes to the Crown and our dues to the Church. We do not attack ranchos and
haciendas.

I am a Black woman. So what? I am the grand niece of Juan de Valladolid, the Black Count, appointed to take care of the affairs of the Black population in an area of the country. That is what counts. Yet here they do not know exactly what to call us. Pardos is fine for me. Or Moreno. The truth is I do not care. What is very important to me is to be called "Señora." Señora, a direct heir of Don Juande Valladolid.

Our family was well respected in Algarve. The Catholic Crown raised Don Juan to the status of Alcalde de los Negros. Their Majesties, Fernando and Isabel, personally conferred such dignity on him. Black Count. That was what we call him at Algarve, the Black Count. He was a rich man –a talented, brave and well intentioned man. He applied the Crown's justice among the Black population.

On the other side, on my father's side, we are Moors. Actually my father's grandfather came from Mali, a very distant country. He was a soldier in the army of a great king, called Mansa Musa. A Mandingo lord.

Mansa Musa was a Muslim, as was my great-grandfather. We are not Muslims any more; bless the Holy Virgin's grace! And it was for that reason, I mean because he was Muslim, that he decided to go on pilgrimage to Mecca. He rode a horse of the finest breed, with luxurious trappings, and crossed the land they call Africa surrounded by a large number of followers, and a train of fifty camels loaded with gold and gifts. He went through a place called... Oh, daughter, let me see, Let me see. I think the name was Walata or Tuat, I am not sure. Five hundred slaves marched ahead with his belongings. He brought so much gold to Egypt that the value fell for many years.

Mansa Musa was a holy man just as your great-great-grand father, Muslim but holy. An observer of the hour of prayer, he and his elders studied the books of law and memorized texts from the Koran. He was generous to the poor. A well-mannered man, he and his followers made a fine impression in Cairo, and were to be remembered for many, many years.

According to our family's tradition, the Mandingo people were Muslims, but they never lost their culture. Musa's favorite meal was pounded millet with milk and honey. The Mandingo women enjoyed a very privileged position, and property was inherited through the mother's side.

And that is the point I wanted to make. Your father had enough money to give your dowry. And you married with dignity. And you got married to that foreigner, that African that I have never been able to accept. I don't mean that he is a bad person. At least he has a good job under the Governor's shadow, with all of those languages he says he can speak. The point is that the Governor is not a good person, so if he is that comfortable with him, well then he is not that nice either.

I mean, you come from a distinguished family. You had no need to marry a pirate. And I will never forgive your father for having consented to this marriage which was like indulging a spoiled child. It was always like that, he really spoiled you.

Anyway, getting back to the case, my great-great-grand father met Es-Saheli, the famous Spanish architect and artist. Es-Saheli's tales awoke his imagination, and aroused in his heart the desire to travel. On his way back from Mecca he managed to convince King Musa to leave him behind to study. Once on his own, he made his way to Granada. After the conquest by Castile and Aragon, that part of the family settled in La Puebla and became Christian.

That's where we get our color from. And look at you. Come let me take a good look. Baby, you are cute! Like your grandmother. My beloved Amachi, who was a beatiful but unpredictable Ibo woman, daughter of a slave from a place called Sahara, I think it is. He was the one that denounced Diego de Andurria's treason to the Spanish Crown. I am not sure exactly what happened. All I know is that he was de Andurria's slave and he denounced his master's treason. Because of this they gave him freedom and authorization to marry a Spanish woman. So my grandmother was born free.

That is the history of our family. We have been the relatives and servants of kings and queens. We have been loyal to Spain. I never imagined my daughter married to an African Portuguese pirate, with those devilish green cat-eyes. For heaven's sake, Portuguese! God help me, a friend of a Governor that should well be burnt, more so than the so called witch women that he burns.

So I claim the right to go home. To go back to my country, to my region. I came to Santo Domingo with your father. Juan, who as the whole Alcino family, was a proud Pardo. We are all proud to be Pardos. We came to work the land. We came to work on the land. The priest at home told us that there was a danger that we might become enslaved. I didn't care. I was completely convinced that we could work our way out and buy our freedom in a few years. We are hard working and honest people, my husband and myself. We hoped to be rich, and that our children would become as distinguished as their ancestors were. So if we had to be enslaved, that would just be a temporary inconvenience.

It didn't happen. And by the Holy Virgin we are lucky. Slavery in this country is a cruel and humiliating thing.

It is almost impossible to believe that a slave master here is free to kill his slave. The "Siete Partidas" –that well establish Ancient Spanish Slave Code is of no use here. The master can starve his slave to death, if he wants to. Slaves cannot take their masters to court. And it is almost impossible for a slave; no matter how hard working he may be, to buy his own liberty, or that of his wife and children. There is no respect for enslaved people, no Christian love. In fact, they are not treated like people.

Your father is very old now. He will die at any moment –that is the truth. Why pretend we don't know that? I do not want my children to end up here in Santo Domingo. I want them to go back to Spain, and become citizens. I have the money. All I need is the Governor's permission to leave the Island, and your husband's consent. In Spain he could enter service with one of the important families, with all those languages that he says he can speak. All I need is the permission; our bones should rest in Granada. Maybe in La Puebla.

Tell your husband to convince the Governor. Things are desperate here, since the "Bozales" –that mob of African slaves revolted and killed the former governor. There have been death penalties even for trying to escape. Pardo people cannot carry firearms any more. All of us are considered Maroons now. But as you know, we are not bozales, we are not run-away slaves. So, daughter, I resent being called that way. My family, as I have explained is distinguishon all sides. We are Pardos. We are Spanish Pardos. Why are we been treated like pagan bozales?

Even the Church has turned against us. And may the Holy Virgin beg forgiveness for me, and may Saint Iago overlook my words if they are wrongly said, but the main responsible is Cardinal Cisneros. According to the parish priest he considers us a threat. He should come and see for himself. We are Black; we are Pardos or Morenos, or whatever they wish to call us. But we are Christians. We are hard working Spanish Christian people. We are not Maroons. We don't live in the "cumbes" and "maniles" as they call the negroes' communal ranches and shanty townships. The Governor and the Cardinal himself can come here to see for themselves. We pay taxes to the Crown and our dues to the Church. We do not attack ranchos and haciendas.

We certainly do not approve of the Maroons' behavior, although the truth be said, the Spaniards over here are not like those at home. I think this Santo Domingo air corrupts the mind and turns people into savages because some of the Señores here are a disgrace to Spain. Take for example Señor Vázquez de la Mancha. I mean, it is true that Lucas helped the rebels get into the governor's house, but Lucas didn't know that they intended to kill him. His only mistake was to let that damn young trouble maker –what is his name? –Juan Bautista, the one the slaves call Primo de Kwami to convince him to open the door. And yet this cruel Vázquez de la Mancha tied the poor man by his hands and feet, each limb to a different horse, and burst him open in front of the whole city. Primo de Kwami got away but dear Lucas is dead. Lucas was not a Bozal. He was a Christian, and his father a Spanish man from Seville.

And now, after all this horror, Vázquez de la Mancha boasts himself as one of Cardinal Cisneros' most faithful friends. But his beard is black, gray and white. And tree-colored beards are only seen on the face of traitors. And may it not be true that the worst pig get the best acorn. If Cisneros and Vázquez de la Mancha are such close friends, the whore and the villain live together.

No, no, give me a chance: this is no scandal, my dear. And I am not lowering my voice, I mean, you want to come around and boss me? Anyway, boiling water cools, always cools. And yes, I know, I know that one should not go to somebody's home to insult him. But, bear with me. Juan de Alcino is old now, very old. Tell your husband to help us to go home. If you don't want to come with us, that's all right, but help us. You shall be blessed. I know that the Governor and your husband are not evil like Cisneros and Vázquez de la Mancha the Inquisitor. Your husband might even be an honest person, and my judgment could be unfair. So may my tears be useful. And please leave me alone, let me cry. May Mary be well served. Blessed is she among women. Amen. And blessed is the fruit of her womb, Jesus. May she pray for us. May Lucas, who all his life was a godly man, rest in peace. May God forgive my chattering. May Saint Iago overlook my evil thoughts. And may my humble petition be granted.

THE BONFIRE

THE bonfire burns in the dark forest. The Leader had summoned them to listen to the songs of the Griot, the poet –depositor of the collective memory, the holder of poetry and of the chronicles that extend way beyond time. He evoked the memory of that which had no beginning. The songs of the Griot has no finale.

THE bonfire burns in the dark forest. The Leader had summoned them to listen to the songs of the Griot, the poet –depositor of the collective memory, the holder of poetry and of the chronicles that extend way beyond time. He evoked the memory of that which had no beginning. The songs of the Griot has no finale.

- But… what about a straight answer?

- Well, before the beginning only Nyame was there.

The Old man was using very strange words. Some thought he was loosing his mind. A lady, listening from the other side of the gathering, commented loud enough so that all of them could hear: "Too much thinking, me 'ole mama use to say, too much thinking will make you slip you mind."

According to his own story, he was captured and enslaved in Arabia. Taking advantage of the trust his master had in him, he escaped, only to be recaptured in Lagos and given as a gift to the Pope.

The problem was, no one in the camp knew about Lagos and the Pope, and they would have ignored him if it was not for the miraculous cure of the Leader's wife which he had performed.

- Exactly what is the point? – the leader asked.

- Well, you have to take into account that Nyame is the Unburnable. Nyame Odomankoma is the Infinite.

The Leader yawned. He had been very patient with the Griot, but his patience had its limits. So he urged him to just get to the point. But, as if under some sort of spell, the poet went on.

- I'm coming, I'm coming. You see. It is He who in time permits the concretion of the kra —person'sunique life-force or Breath of God, given before birth, to develop one's potential.

As his wife approached and murmured something in his ear, the Leader yawned again. It was really becoming more than he could take. The Old Man went on to declare them direct heirs of the builders of gigantic pyramids of which no one had heard before.

- Those are the great works of Kemet, on the other side of the Sahara.

- I am trying to follow you —the Leader said —but I can't understand the relation between Nyame, Kemet, the problem that I have placed before you and your songs. I believe that we have to decide, because there is great confusion between us and that is not good.

- Well, dear Leader —the Old Man continued with great reverence —the problem is our sunsum.

- What?

-Our Sum summ the Soul of the group, the communal soul.

-What are you taking about?

- Nyame, He Who Was Not Created. He had no father or mother.

The listeners broke out into laughter, and that eased the tension a little bit.

By now the Leader had on his face an expression of desperation. The people standing by, who could have been termed a "congregation", were glancing at the Griot, trying in vain to make sense out of his songs.

There were a lot of people at the meeting that night. Much more than expected —considering it was not a jam.

It was not a party, but a meeting of people about the fundamental questions of the spirit, and the thousand traditions of which they were now heirs.

- So we have Ra, and Nyame, and Olodumare...

Another old man from the very back of the group shouted, "shut him up and go on with the damn meeting."

-You can shut me up, the Griot said, but you will still have to face the sunsum question. For in every community you have Anansi the Spider: An expression of God, who on becoming a trickster lost grace introducing treachery and evil. There is always a traitor. So we need a common sunsum to keep us together.

The Griot went silent for a moment. The Leader's Sister then got permission to speak.

- Ah –she said -that is exactly what is happening here. My uncle, Kwame's brother, the Second, died during the mutiny on the slave ship, not by the hands of the White man who foolishly blasted them to pieces, but by the hands of his own cousin. So it was betrayal that cost me this wound on my leg, and cost us the lives of many brave men and women. So, it was Anansi. Now I know it. It was Anansi!

- Come on, Aunt –another young voice shouted –tell them. Let them never forget that it was we Yayahs that organized the rebellion.

- But you don't have to worry –the Old Man said, and ignoring the young boy's comment, went on to tell her in a triumphant tone:

–God placed Brother Chameleon in his space.

The Griot fell asleep, having consumed the energy that he managed to steal from age, giving place to a younger voice.

- I was a captive for ten years, and I was baptized in the Catholic Church and in these lands no other religion is allowed. The Old Man's story is the same story I have heard the White priests preach in the Church. It is the same story, only that over here God is not called Nyame; he is called

God the Father and I believe Adwenka is like Jesus Christ. And then there is The Holy Spirit... I don't know if that is the Breath of God, or Life-Force or what...But it is not that different.

All were now attentive to the new voice.

- In this land, any one that practices our religion is condemned as a witch. The medicine women are also considered witches. And they burn them; they murder them with lashes.

- So what is the point, young man?

The Leader emphasized young, because it was very audacious on the part of this young man to speak in front of the older men without having been authorized.

- I am a devotee of Saint John the Baptist –he said, as murmurs swept all the way through the camp. My family is from the Congo. So for me Saint John the Baptist is Shangóthe Yoruba god of war, lightening and thunder.

One of the old ladies burst out laughing and was soon followed by others in the gathering, until the sound of joy filled the forest.

- Now Leader –another of the ladies said –let me get this straight. You are a very wise Yayah man, you will know better. This boy is from the Congo. He is not Yoruba. But he is a devoted follower of Shangó.

- Yes Ma'am –the young man replied –you see, I am Black. A Black African. Saint John the Baptist from the Congo, he too is Black. So he is our Saint.

- A Black what?

- A Black African...

- A Black African. I wonder what that is. And how did you get Shangó into this?

The Leader stood up and beckon to them to be silent.

- How did you come to know about John the Baptist Congo?

- I was named after him.

- So your name is Saint John.

- No, my name is Juan Bautista.

- I see. Well this young man has spoken with wisdom. He said we all are Black Africans. I am a Black African.

The gathering went silent, and stood almost in awe, as attentive as they could be, over this unexpected approval.

- We must accept that we are all Africans. And we should tell that to the Children. Tell them about John Baptist Congo.

It was a diverse lot. Their faces anointed with palm oil, shinning in the light of the bonfire, all of them together.

- Let me get this straight –the woman bravely replied – what is this thing about being Black Africans?

- Exactly what were we… am…let's say, twice my fingers ago. Let's say, that many months ago. What were we?

- What were we?

- Human beings…said an elderly man who just wanted to be funny.

- Ah, said the Leader, Human beings. What human beings? They all looked at each other, not getting the point. But they knew that there was more coming. For whenever the Leader adopted his solemn kingly posture, there was always much more to be expected.

He stood up tall, his shaft in his left hand, the sword, taken from the last captain that ventured into their Maroon territory, hung firmly from his waist; the voice, the special bellow-like voice with which he spoke and the commanding right hand gesticulation.

- You sound like the Old Man now.

- Do I? Well then he was right. Some of us were forced to go around the Tree of Forgetfulness, weren't we?

- Yeah…

- And after we escaped from the ship, some of us did manage to spill liquor under the Tree of Foundation, didn't we?

- Yeah…

- And you gave thanks to the Orishas who are the Guardians of the Samanfo-

-The more you speak, the more you sound like the Griot. What the rooster is "Samanfo".

-The common lore of the people, including the ancestors, the living and the unborn, their culture, their traditions. You know that a person is never really dead.

- In the name of Olorun –the first old man said.

- Yeah…

- In the name of Yahweh, God of Abraham –the Ethiopian said.

- Yeah…

- In the name of Allah –said the one they called Teacher of the Law.

- Yeah…

- In the name of Nyame, God Almighty.

- Yeah…

- In the name of Mulungu, the one that put order in chaos.

- Yeah…

- In the name of Jesus –Juan Bautista shouted.

- So… you were all people, Yayah, Sumanis, and Banyoros… people. Weren't you?

- Yeah…

- Well, how come there are no white-skinned people among you?

Silence fell on the gathering. They gradually lifted their eyes, taking a good look at each other. The Mandingo people were black. The Ebo people were black. The Wolof people were black. The Yayah people were black. The Fulahghi people were black. The Ashanti people were black. The Brong people were black. All Bantus were black. Sumanis, Banyoros, all as black as the Iwe people and the Fanti people. People, people. All Black, Black, Black.

- Young Juan Bautista is right –the Leader said, but by now it was an absolutely banal observation, and yet he went on anyway with a strong conviction in his voice –we are Black. Let me declare in the name of my Ancestors, in the name of Kwame my grandfather; let me declare that John Baptist Congo is our Saint. Our African Saint.

The drums broke out in sound applause that changed into laughter and then into dances. And indeed the stars had long gone from the skies. But as the poet said, it's always darkest just before dawn.

YANGÁ

(QDM. Detail statue to Yanga).

The drums took over the Mexican
air and told the legend: San
Lorenzo is a free territory.
Slavery has been abolished in
Yangaland. San Lorenzo de Los
Negros is free.

YANGÁ sat under the big tree in front of what he now called home. The tree and a big rock presided over the yard, where his people would gather whenever summoned to discuss military or community matters, to celebrate or to gossip.

He brushed away the fly that insisted on sharing the piece of sugar cane he was about to chew. A sudden fresh afternoon gust did the rest and the fly desisted. He lifted his eyes to take a good look at his stronghold, which the Spaniards termed "palenque." His hut was near the tree, and there were about eighty others widely dispersed and hidden in the bushes. Still, deeper into the Rio Blanco jungle, there were more and more palenques, each with its rebel population, each self sufficient; ready to defend the self-declared freedom, to counterattack and to loot.

-NI KU TÚ –sounds from a drum in drum-coded language interrupted the thick silence of the Veracruz jungle.

The gust left familiar sounds that caught his attention briefly; there were these sounds from distant drums carrying messages. Precise messages, according to a code adopted and carefully taught-up by his Head Drummer, Martin Fang. All of the officials had to learn the language of the drums, and each of the captains had his own personal code, so that the messages could be directed to all or specifically to one of the authorities. He listened for a while, but the sounds went with the gust. Or maybe it was his imagination, or his anxiety.

The struggle was at a crucial moment. They had attacked the Spaniards at the outskirts of Veracruz. Camino Real. The main road leading from the Port to Mexico had been blocked and harassed for a week, until troops were brought in to reinforce the defense system of Veracruz. Yangá and his men then moved out of the area, followed by the Spanish troops.

They led the enemy into their own territory according to plans. Skirmish after skirmish, in an exasperating game of hit and run, disperse and regroup, attack and retreat. The Spaniards at first were delighted by what seemed easy victories, but as the days went by they began to realize that the flight of the Maroons was by no means a signal of defeat, for as they tried to follow them to their palenques, they had followed roads that led nowhere, ditches that were deadly traps, stones that fell mysteriously off the mountains directly onto the troops, and the annoying beat of the drums.

Now, they had laid down their conditions to the Spanish Government —a place to call their own; a place where they could settle down, to buy and to sell, and to teach the children the art and craft of living.

According to the messenger, the sturdy and pretentious Fray Juan Pérez, the Spanish King wanted an agreement. It seemed to Yangá that there was some major danger pending over Veracruz, because at one moment Fray Juan Pérez suggested that the agreement should in any case include three points: no more looting or attacks on the roads and farms, the return of runaway slaves to their rightful masters and the disposition of the Maroons to defend Veracruz in case of an attack by a third party.

Yangá's wife, whose name he could not pronounce, and who for that reason he had renamed Huajaquita, interrupted his musing and brought him back to reality. She brought food —boiled plantain, corn-cakes and meat.

As usual she could not resist the temptation to caress his hair. Yangá slapped her on the rump. She put on the silly smile that he loved dearly, and walked away slowly. Yangá could not take his eyes away from her long thick black-blue hair, her dark Zambo color, and her body, built as African women were built, with the same dignity that in his memory distinguished women of the land that, as someone suggested, must have been the territory of the "Brongs", or "Brams" or whatever they were called. But he did not remember the name of the land. It was his mother's face, stricken in anguish, and his father's voice that came again and again, especially when Huajaquita chose to call him by the secret name that he had only revealed to her.

Huajaquita sat on another stone some distance from him. He had not succeeded in getting her to sit beside him, or for that matter, eating with him. Her admiration for him seemed so great, that she preferred to sit in reverential awe and watch him eat.

He loved her dearly, and just could not keep his hands off her body. There had been some sort of mysterious attraction from the first day. Martin Fang told him that people had twin souls, and that maybe that was the explanation of his uncontrollable attraction to Huajaquita.

The first time he saw her he was on the run, chassed by a pack of hounds and a Spanish battalion. He was confused: his responsibility was to distract the battalion while his men took refuge in the woods. He had successfully managed to make them follow him, and had followed the usual procedure. He had crossed the stream several times, but it didn't work – the dogs kept coming.

He was very tired, feeling embarrassed and discouraged, when he finally headed for the big river. There was only one possible crossing place and he hated having to lead the Spaniards to that place. But he had no alternative. The risk was great. So he ran to the river and dashed into the water.

Now, as Kojo puts it, dogs are dogs, they are not smarter than men. So he got over to the other bank and advanced inland. After a considerable walk, he felt safe enough to sit down, and chew some weed. This custom he had adopted from the native people. He needed the rest. Hoping that his band had made it safely out of the reach of the Spanish army, he fell asleep.

He would have slept for a long while, had it not been for the dogs. They were on his trail again, barking. He leaped to his feet almost in a fit. "It can't be" he told himself. But it was.

His body, as if possessed by a leopard, dashed through the jungle at great speed. Speed that was it. The dogs could follow but not the Spaniards, clad as they were in iron breasts and helmets.

He had to keep far ahead, out of the reach of the muskets and pistols. Lances were not effective against the iron breast. It had to be an unexpected body to body struggle. In that sense he and his men enjoyed superiority. So he could take on a whole battalion, led by a pack of fierce hounds.

As he dashed further into the jungle alongside the Rio Blanco, the dense vegetation gave way to an opening, at the end of which were a few huts.

He stopped briefly, stooped, and opened his mouth to take in some fresh air, his heart pounding. Behind him the dogs went on barking. Instinctively he ran away from the clearing only to find himself facing a cliff. There seemed to be no way out. He felt like a cornered wildcat. No way out. The Land of Brongs was distant. This was Rio Blanco. His options were very clear. He could face the dogs and the Spanish battalion. He had his spears, and a short sword. He could kill the dogs; they were no match for him compared to the wild animals his ancestors faced back home. But the dogs had masters. He could give in to them, but he had promised, like so many Africans had, that "before I'd be a slave, I'll rather be buried in my grave, and then go back to the land of the Ancestors." He could leap off the cliff, indeed. But then there was the profound wisdom of one of the old African Maroons who had fought in the band of Francisco de la Matosa. One of the leaders of the rebellion in Guatulco had hanged himself to avoid being caught by the Spaniards. The old man did not approve of his conduct.

- Listen to me, Yangá. Listen to me carefully. This man no hero. No hero at all. Dead man can't cut tiger-throat.

No, he would not leap off the cliff. At that very desperate moment, while the dogs came closer, a girl came running by, heading directly for the cliff. She beckoned and he ran instinctively after her. He saw her climb over the side of the cliff and followed. He fell into a cave and before he could react there were some six spears pointing at his throat. The girl said something and they quickly led him through the cavities into an opening. He now faced the man who seemed to be the chief.

He wondered if this was one of the Aztecs he used to hear about. In that case, he was a dead man, since prisoners of war were sacrificed to the Aztec gods. So he had escaped from the Valley of Death only to fall into the dungeon. At least it would be a more dignified death

The girl seemed to have authority, for she spoke directly to the Chief, explaining the situation. Whatever she said must have satisfied the Chief because he ordered them to let him loose.

They then gave him for the first time what is now his favorite drink: thick chocolate with hot pepper.

The Chief seemed to welcome him. The men looked boldly at each other.

They were a strange lot. Some looked like pure native people, others were clearly Africans. Some, like the girl who had saved his life, were evidently mix-blooded Afro-Native American. Zambos. In fact, many of the children were Zambos.

Before he could figure out his situation one of the men that had been observing him started jumping madly.

- It is Yangá –he shouted. In his glee he had been speaking in his African tongue, a language Yangá spoke when a child, almost as fluently as his own. The people laughed at him. Finally he made himself understood to them.

- This man is Yangá.

And not being able to control himself, went down on his knees in front of the newcomer, and told him, in his deeply Africanized Spanish:

- Me tu sclavo.

A sudden silence went through the camp. The Chief came closer, and took a long, long look.

-Yangá? –he seemed to ask.

Yangá raised his hand in salutation.

- Yes, me Yangá –he said politely. And turning to the African, "Get up, me no take slaves."

The Chief backed away in awe, and all of the others stepped backward, as if performing a ritual. The Chief then took a jade necklace he was wearing and moving close to Yangá placed it around his neck

- We have waited a long time to meet our leader -he said.

- NDÁN… ya, ya, yan…yangá ya, ya, yan…Yangá. Ya, ya, yan…yangá, ya, ya, yan…-the drums were now beating steadily and clearly. It was a message for him. He looked at his wife. But this time, he did not look at the woman. He turned to the warrior.

Huajaquita came close and was about to say something but he signaled her to be silent. She listened to the rhythmic sounds, and although she could not understand the meaning, she knew the message was for the leader. She reached over and handed his drum to him, as he turned his ears to the wind. Without hesitation he took the drum and beat back. In no time he was surrounded by several of his top officials.

- A prisoner… no not a prisoner, a messenger was located… Spanish.

Yangá at first could not understand the situation.

- Kill him –he pounded. The order went over the bushes. "Kill him."

But the answer came back from the Captain.

- Important message from king. Kill him after? Yangá let the drum-words sink deeply into his mind.

- All right: bring him in. Travel at dark.

"NI KU TÚ... yan, yan, yan...Yangá. Yan, yan, yan... Yangá. Yan, yan, yan...Yangá...

He went back to his meditations as the shadows fell.

He remembered that very distant day. It was in broad daylight that the watchman fell asleep. The Spanish battalion got very close to them and they were forced to run for their lives frantically. From the top of the tree where he took refuge he saw them heading directly to the road that led to his Palenque. He knew from experience what that meant. He was there when they captured Francisco de la Matosa's Palenque. The Spaniards burnt the sixty huts and seized the crops and destroyed what they could not take with them. So he got down from the tree and ran desperately toward the enemy. As soon as he was close enough, he made himself seen and shouted in a rather boyish and awkward Spanish that they should surrender.

- Mi Yangá ordena rendirse castellanos...

The Spanish official turned around and ordered the battalion to capture him. He faced them for a while and then took off into the bushes, shouting insults to the official in his very best Castilian.

The Spanish officer seemed to take it personally and chased him all day, until he accidentally ran into the hideout of Huajaquita's people, and was taken into safety and became instantaneously "The Leader" who they had been waiting for.

Night had just spread itself over San Lorenzo when he felt the usual urge to bury himself in the warmth of Huajaquita's skin. He led her into the darkness of the hut.

- The moon is not in the right position –she said, faithful
to the traditions of her people. Sex had to do with the
position of the moon. The day was proper but not the right
hour to have strong healthy children.

- Damn the moon –he said. She laughed.

- Esina Nulai, she said, the sprits will put a curse on my
womb if you keep on with your foolish talk.

But Yangá could not be stopped. He expected morning to
be the dawn of a new day for them. The beginning of a New
Life. The Palenque, his African Palenque, would become a
Mexican African Palenque.

The couple collided like the merging of two violent rivers.
Sighs and roars filled the hut as they rubbed and forced their
bodies together, trying hard to share the same space. For
having their bodies share the same space is the utmost dream
of lovers.

Yes, that day was now distant. After the Spaniards
destroyed and left the place, (the Amerindians communicated
with mouth signals) they came out of their hiding place.
Yangá discovered that that was not their home: it was a fake.
The real Palenque was half a day's walk from the caves.

Being the leader now, he got the chief to assign some men
to him, including Green Walker, the native expert guide who
led them over the mountain through the thick vegetation
directly to the only possible place where the Spaniard could
cross the river.

His men were searching for him, and were glad to see
him as usual, as they joined forces. Yangá ordered them to
bury the bodies of the Spanish soldiers. He wanted them to
disappear completely. He then went to his own Palenque and
summoned the men.

- We should establish our own village –he told them –
settle down and become a people.

The men said he was crazy like a bat. To settle in one
place was just the same as surrendering. They would be

captured and led back to the farms and mines, back to slavery. But Yangá insisted, asking them to join Huajaquita's people.

In the end, the majority agreed, more out of loyalty to the Leader than out of conviction. But as he moved towards the caves next day some eighty men, fifty women and about twenty children followed.

Love, as usual, was great. But, he did not sleep well. There was this excitement in his mind. Before dawn he wrapped himself in the poncho that Huajaquita had made for him, and went out to stand under his tree. Just to think.

The guard saluted respectfully but Yangá was in not a greeting mode that morning, and could not bring himself to give a proper reply. He sort of grunted, and went over to wet the bushes.

He then settled under the tree for a while, trying hard to continue his musing. But the urge to be with Huajaquita was still strong. He headed back to the hut and into the corner where his wife slept. Unrestrained, he tried again to share the same space with her.

- Damn crazy cold African –she protested, and then did what she always did –bury her fingers deeply into his hair.

- I think that the messenger will bring us good news tomorrow –he whispered, his man-ness locked firmly into her woman-ness.

- We will have a place for our children. And our people can teach the art of pottery and weaving to the next generation.

- Well, we will live in Yangaland –she panted back, as the energetic fluids burst through their bodies forcefully, compelling them to fill the hut with the everlasting and universal grunts of life.

- I love you Esinan Nulai –she said, as she laid back to rest, and fell easily into the comfort of sleep. He lay sleeping beside her for a while. He loved her just as she was. Shy when she wanted to be; but a brave, valiant warrior, ready to take her place in the battlefield. She could send her Spanish enemies home to their Lord in the twinkle of an eye, and feel good about it. Her large, dark eyes, her cool Zambo complexion. Her body that made him remember vaguely women gathered on a ship's deck. Her cunning ways of love that so exited him; her dream of building a new nation, where they could teach the arts and crafts of living to the next generation. Her devotion. He could not imagine life without her anymore. She had become a part of his very existence.

He went back to sit under the tree, his poncho on his back, and watched the skies go from black to dark gray. The sun whitened the clouds gradually and filled the skies with a million yellowish tones. The guards changed and Fang, the Head Drummer, came to sit in front of the tree, just in case.

- Summon the officials –he told him, and went back into his hut.

Huajaquita was already on foot.

- I need your help –he told her–the officers will be here very soon. We should offer food.

- I'll get help from the other women. Don't worry.

Yangá met with the Chief who was now his First Officer, and they went to the stream to wash and to chat freely. In fact, the First Officer was Huajaquita's younger brother, so the men considered themselves brothers. They made a great team. It was through contact with them that he had come to believe that it was possible to become a people, by forcing the Spaniards to negotiate. Now he was expecting good news.

By the time they gathered around the tree, gourds of chocolate with hot pepper and corn cakes were waiting. The men arrived gradually, ate and took their places, all there, ready to listen to Yangá's word.

The drums announced that the messenger would arrive at early morning. So Yangá explained that it was the answer from the King.

- If the message is positive we will become a peaceful people. Right there in San Lorenzo.

There was a lot of excitement in the Palenque when the messenger finally walked into the yard, escorted by the Head Guard. It was Fray Juan Pérez.

- Hello. There is the powerful Black Captain, strong as usual —he said in a somewhat mocking tone.

One of Yangá's men came rushing with a fine stool in one hand, a walking rod and a shawl in the other. It was Kojo. A few steps behind, his wife Ekua kept up his pace. She had a second stool in her hand, much less elaborated than the one Kojo carried.

He was the spiritual leader of the community. He placed the stool under the tree, and his wife placed the other a couple steps away.

- Things should be done properly- he sort of rebuked Yangá who respectfully smiled and bowed to his elder. He then took seat on the stool, the shawl over his shoulder, the rod in his right hand.

Kojo signaled to Fray Juan Perez, who took his place on the other stool. Kojo then recited a salutation:

Kerapa, let there be health and let there be life

Let the Leader be wise and good hearted

All good to the people, to the women, to the Natives living among us.

Let the women be able to bear children

And let the men accumulate riches for their families.

And if any dare to wish us wrong

May such wrong be multiplied and to them bestowed.

Fray Pérez stood. And as if possessed by some strange spirit, shouted:

- There is only one God. God Almighty. To Him be the praise and the glory.

No one understood the reason for such sudden rapture. They stared at him until he sat down.

- Is the news good?
- Yes. Luis de Velasco is ready to sign an agreement with you. You can establish yourselves at San Lorenzo. History will speak of San Lorenzo de Los Negros, I guess. You are expected to be free servants of the King and good children of your Mother the Church. So if you are ready to sign...
- Give the papers to Juan Bautista –he said, pointing to the official translator. Juan Bautista spoke several African and Native languages, and was fluent in Latin, and Castilian. He was a runaway Pardo slave who had been recaptured. He was eventually persuaded to become a priest by Fray Antonio, an idealistic monk. But when he discovered that the children of single women were considered "bastards" and for that reason could not be ordained, he went off to join the Maroons.

Juan Bautista read out load:

- The Council understands that in the land known as Rio Blanco a good number of Blacks have taken arms and have lost respect for the legally established authorities...

Yangá braced himself, preparing for the insults. He was now too old to tolerate any more nonsense. If after the usual beating around the bush which seem to delight the Spaniards there was no real agreement, it would be Fray Juan Perez's last day.

Juan Bautista read on:

- So do what you can to bring peace, and accept his conditions, that is, that they can establish themselves peacefully without arms at San Lorenzo, that they are declared free, that land will be allotted to them so that they can settle down and occupy themselves in the production of food and other useful occupations, with the warning that from here on they shall return any runaway slave to his natural owner.

- Give the man a gourd of chocolate and some tobacco. Tonight we will feast. Tomorrow I sign the papers and we take the Father back.

The drums took over the Mexican air and told the legend: San Lorenzo is a free territory. Slavery has been abolished in Yangaland. San Lorenzo de Los Negros is free.

JUAN BAUTISTA'S STORY

His back, broad, strong; his waistline, his buttocks. I stood in awe, looking at his body, as he, having heard me calling, turned around to get his trousers. ... I knew he saw me, although he pretended not to. My face was burning, my heart pounding wildly.

I will never forget that sunny morning. It had rained the night before, and as the sun hit the damp grass, one could smell the fragrance of life surging. I came walking up the river bank, with my jug of water firmly on my head. I was singing a tune that my father always sang, repeating the words he used, without really knowing the meaning. I was wearing a skirt, wrapped and tied firmly around my waist. My feet were bare, and a loose blouse hardly covered my breasts.

As I came to the top of the rise, I felt eyes watching me. I turned around, but there was no one in sight. So I decided to hurry. As I approached the house, I called out to mother, "I'm back" –which as was agreed upon in my family was the proper thing to do in this case. Mother came out on the porch with her pistol ready to blow off the intruder's head.

She raised her eyes over my head and asked "Who's that?" and it was then that I turned to look again and saw him. My heart leaped and pounded out of control. I put the jug on the ground, and walked over to stand beside my mother. We both stared at the stranger. I had never seen a man like that before. The dark bronze skin of his bare chest shining in the sun, as if to say, decorated with just the right amount of hair. He was well groomed. He was wearing pants, very much like the Spaniards did.

He came directly to us, ignoring the gun, and asked if he could buy some breakfast. His name was Juan Bautista.

Mama, without hesitation, which was uncharacteristic of her, said he could, if he was willing to take whatever was served. It was not long after that Juan Bautista was eating. He laughed a lot, showing his white teeth, placed evenly in the dark purple gum. I could not take my eyes off his thick, well aligned lips, juicy, fresh like a sweet slice of orange.

Mama caught me staring and slapped me across the bottom. I blushed and turned away for a moment, but then she asked where he came from, and It was impossible for me not to look at him as he began to tell his story.

He was born on a hacienda, near Coro in Colombia. His father, Primo de Kwami, had been a mine worker at Buria and Nigua, sites of Colombian Maroons. One day the headmaster got angry over some minor incident related to a broken tool, accused his father, had him whipped and kept him tied in the sun without water all day.

Five of his fellow enslaved Africans managed to free him before dark and then decided to run away. One of the enslaved, named Miguel, was identified as the leader by the overseer and punished with fifty lashes. The overseer promised to castrate Miguel next morning. This provoked the rebellion of the enslaved, and led by Miguel and his father they got rid of the guards and overseers, and went to the camps to get their families. The word went around fast, and by noon Miguel found himself as head of some eight hundred men, women and children.

They went to the Jirafara people and negotiated an agreement with them. There they established the original Cumbe, and fortified the village properly. Miguel was named king by the council, and his wife Huida became queen.

- For two years Cumbe resisted, but the Spaniards were so infuriated with us that they did not rest until Cumbe was taken and destroyed.

They then faked King Miguel and his wife's detention and execution. But White men can't kill spirit. So when the pearl workers of Marga Island rose to rebellion, they were led by this very same Mother Queen, with all her strong powers. And although the authorities captured and punished the enslaved, year after year the Maroons established more cumbes under the glorious spiritual leadership of Miguel and Huida. My father went with them, with King Miguel and his wife, all over the territory. The Spaniard announced his death again and again, but the proof that they never were able to kill them was the fact that the number of cumbes grew every year.

Finally Miguel did leave his body, reincarnated, and was named Domingo. A rebellious boy he was. Even in his mother's womb he made trouble. His grandmother was a cook on the hacienda, so that was how Domingo Biyojo became the godson of Pedro de la Granda, the owner of the Hacienda. In fact, his grandmother had a very close relationship with the Hacendado.

One night Domingo was caught in the Spanish section of the town, and was accused of attempting to steal cornflour. The Council had him severely flogged, with forty lashes and don Pedro was fined one peso for not keeping his slave properly safeguarded at night. The peso infuriated his master, who from there on treated Domingo very harshly and told him that he would have to pay back the peso through extra work.

His uncle Juan de Dios Kwame Yaya was a good carpenter, and used to work in town. He could keep a part of his earnings and give the rest to his master. So he came to some agreement with don Pedro, paid the peso and asked permission to use the boy as another hand. But don Pedro was blunt:

- No, I am not going to do like some of my peers, breaking the law. Your place in the caste system is that of a tercerón. So you are on a White man's job according to the law. We tolerate you because you are a good worker, and were already a carpenter when the law was decreed by his Majesty.

Domingo overheard the conversation. He knew that the whole country had been developed by industrious people like his uncle Juan de Dios Kwame Yaya, and his grandfather "Tata" Marco Antonio Luango Yaya, whose agricultural skills and know-how were well known. He thought about the songs and poems and the stories with which the nurses and nannies had nurtured the White Creole children. He remembered Mateo Jesús Bambara and his skill for numbers, and he knew that don Pedro de la Granda depended almost completely on his talents for commerce. He knew that a large part of Miss de la Granda's furniture and jewelry —just like that of the majority of the rich women in town —came from the hands of Diego Banyoro Yaya Asante. And what about the weaving by Pedro Benin Sumani whom the Africans called Popo? And his sister's Old Mother María Ayobi? Life would certainly be tasteless in this country if they had not been able to benefit from the skills of the Africans and their descendants.

But, since early youth, Domingo found himself excluded from Spanish society. It didn't matter that, in the caste system, he was a cuarterón. He watched his master brand the new comers with a hot iron stamping a proud DLG on their arms. He watched as his master turned harsher when his youngest son got married secretly to Salvadora, a Mulatto girl, with the complicity of a liberal priest, turning herself into a shameless "salto pa'tra" a backward leap in the caste-race system. Don Pedro was convinced that his daughters would not be able to marry with men of his rank, free from what he termed "the contamination of Guinea race", and that his own descendants would not even be able to dress properly, since the law prohibited Mestizos to dress like White Spaniards.

Domingo could remember how he cried bitterly when his aunt was caught stealing codfish. She was pregnant and could not live without salt fish. She was placed belly down with a hole in the ground to "avoid hurting the baby" he heard an old lady say, held in her place, stripped and given six lashes by

the overseer. Then the old Black lady went over to bathe her
back with vinegar and salt water to keep her skin from being
poisoned.

He loved his aunt and could not understand why she
should be lashed so savagely for a piece of fish, since every
one knew that she was a perfectly honest person, and that her
sudden craving for salt fish was nothing more that a result of
her pregnancy.

Domingo raged when don Pedro cut his best friend's
Tomasito's nose for coming too close to De la Granda's young
daughter in a rather foolish attempt to get a better smell of
her perfume. And he raged harshly when they recaptured
José Dolores, who had eloped with Marta, a young girl from
the neighboring hacienda. He had managed to keep himself
on the run for some months, but was caught trying to buy
tobacco in town. José Dolores was led through the town
jingling bells and whipped orderly. He was given a hundred
lashes and left with his hands tied together and his feet
in irons all day, so that the entire population could see the
destiny of all rebellious slaves.

Finally Domingo got fed up with raging.He marked
the year 1603 and organized a rebellion. He was confirmed
heir of the Old African Kingdoms by the council, and given
a new name: King Benkos. He then established his own
Palenque, where hundreds of Africans and their descendants
took refuge, to have their day, to loot and take vengeance, but
above all, to taste dignity and freedom. Domingo fought for
thirteen years, until his Palenque was finally given the status
of a free territory, under the protection of His Majesty the
King of Spain, and his people given the right to dress like
the Spaniards, and Domingo could carry arms in public. But
it was not long before Domingo was accused of conspiracy,
captured by the authorities and hanged.

Juan Bautista finished his breakfast with Domingo's
death. He politely suggested the possibility of staying for a

day's rest. Mama told him that the matter would have to be discussed later with her husband.

Shortly after noon, he went to the pool to bath. Home seemed empty to me, as if his presence were a normal part of our daily life, or rather, the reality that our cabin lacked. So when Papa came and Mama told me to call him, I was glad to obey.

In our small Panamanian county we did not have many visitors. Strangers were a rare species, and for that reason the subject of our delight. I imagine that he was about the forth or fifth stranger that I had actually seen. I ran toward the stream, calling out his name, which sounded like music to me. I dashed down the bank, only to get a glimpse of naked beauty. I stopped abruptly and went silent. His back, broad, strong; his waistline, his buttocks. I stood in awe, looking at his body, as he, having heard me calling, turned around to get his trousers. I could not help noticing how gifted he was.

Reluctantly I backed away slowly. I knew he saw me, although he pretended not to. My face was burning, my heart pounding wildly.

- Hey- he shouted back- I'm coming.

At the top of the bank I waited until he came close and then walked ahead. I could not face him with all my being in flame.

Father was delighted to meet Juan Bautista. He had heard so much about Palenque San Basilio, and wanted to know the end of the story.

To hang King Benkos turned out to be a big mistake on the part of the Spaniards. The people then organized themselves into "cuagros", which were self sustained military units, integrated with an equal number of men and women. Some of the leaders were pure Africans. Newcomers who brought with them knowledge that the local Black population lacked, about how to govern a nation at war. Kikongo people, with common cultural traits they could share. Kimbumdu people, with their tales and bravado. The Spanish army could not suppress them this time. Because of that they sent one Bishop Casiani to negotiate, and when they reached an agreement, the Governor of Cartagena himself signed it.

My father leaped to his feet, spilling Mama's hot soup all over the place.

- Are you telling me that the Palenque is free?

- There are no enslaved people in San Basilio now, and no Spaniards, except the priests. No White person can come into our region without the permission of our leaders.

- God be blessed! God bless your ancestors! Nothing lasts forever. Gye Nyame! No one has lived long enough to have seen when it started; no one will live long enough to see it end. Great God. Except God!

- Blessed be the Virgin Mary! –Mama said, and broke out into tears, and added –my grandmother died at San Basilio.

- Palenqueros pay taxes to the Spanish Crown like everybody else, but we elect our own authorities just like we used to do at home.

- At home?

- Back in Africa.

My father went to the river to wash himself, then got his nkumbi drum, the maracas that he bought from the Caribbean man that passed through our village some time ago, and his guitar, and we all went over to our neighbor's cabin. The Santiagos as usual welcomed us. They were very happy to meet Juan Bautista Congo. Every one was.

Word was sent out that we would have a cumba party that night, to celebrate the presence of our visitor and to tell the story of free San Basilio. The Native families also came along with drums and flageolets.

I will always remember that night. Let me put it this way –I will remember the rapture, the magic of being in the bosom by life itself, for while my parents slept their drinks away, frankly speaking, I gave myself to Juan Bautista and took him into my body. And although he had to move on, as he continued his mission, to tell the truth, his love has kept me going all these years.

LITTLE ANTONIO FROM PALMARES

(QDM. Detail statue to Zumbi dos Palmares)
Ganga is a genuine leader. He is truly concerned about his people. And we would have had peace if it was **not** for Juan Bautista and **your** beloved Francisco Zumbi

LITTLE Antonio took one last glance at himself in the mirror. His sandals fit properly on his feet. White pants and jacket, in contrast with his dark ash-like skin. He touched his golden colored buttons as if to give it all the final wave of elegance. And, oh, his hair! He had to comb his hair again. Satisfied, he walked solemnly to the door to receive the visitor.

- Father - he saluted and fell to his knees.

- Little Antonio. Are you behaving properly?

- Yes Father, you know me.

He rose up and took the priest's coat and walking cane.

- Hope you are not taking part in those secret ceremonies in the woods. Juan Bautista is not a saint, not a Christian Saint. He is a worthless Yayah. Zumbi is not from the Congo, he was born right here in Brazil, and the Church does not approve of your primitive African rites. You are not a pagan any more. You are a Christian, Antonio, you must behave like one.

Little Antonio forced himself to smile.

- Father, your words are sacred to me.

- Well, I am glad to hear that. You are a very lucky lad. Your master and his family are very kind to you. Be obedient to them.

The priest started walking firmly. It was obvious that he knew the way.

- God bless you Father –Little Antonio managed to murmur, as he kept up with the minister's pace. –Don Jâo is waiting for you in the library.

As the priest came through the door, Don Jâo stood up and extended his hands as if to embrace him. Both men patted each other's shoulders merrily.

- Here's for your buts, Father Elías –Don Jâo offered a seat, using a somewhat rude but very typical expression, and they sat down comfortably.

Little Antonio asked if he could be of service and was told to bring some drinks.

- This is a special occasion. This Holy Man had forgotten the road to my home. But now he is back. We have to celebrate.

Little Antonio went out in a rush. He ordered wine and cheese from the kitchen and hurriedly went back to his post at the door, just in time to listen to the beginning of the conversation.

- It's about your behavior Don Jâo.
- My behavior! Father, for heaven's sake, what do you expect from me? What more can I do?
- Your wife is not happy with your conduct. You seem to have a notable weakness for women.

Don Jâo laughed out loud. The cheese and wine came, and Little Antonio set the table elegantly. He poured two cups from the decanter, and placed the plate of cheese within reach. He then bowed and went back to his post at the door.

- Me with women! You know what, Father? I think my wife is crazy. I think she is going nuts. Maybe she needs to go back to Portugal. Guess she needs to drink the water of her land for a while. Then she will see how good life is for her here in Brazil, and then she will appreciate her husband.

- You are not sticking to the point. You seem to be trying to get away, but I won't let you. I am taking about your maid. The Mulatto girl.

Don Jâo burst out in a loud laughter that went on too long and ended in a vigorous cough. He then took a big drink.

- Father, let me be frank with you. I have been a good husband. It is true that I was born in Angola, and raised in Brazil. But I have more land, gold and silver than the majority of the Portuguese nobles. Let me put it this way: my wife could get a husband with royal blood and womanly manners. What is better for her, Father? She has a husband that makes her feel what love is like. She is mother to four children, two sons and two daughters. She is a rich woman, and her children will be rich; richer, much richer than she could ever dream to be if she had one of those Portuguese petty princes.

- It's not about your wealth, it's about Lourdes.

- I can't understand this woman. I have been a good husband and father. She goes around handing out my riches in charitable works. And yet, she is very ungrateful.

- She is just jealous. She says you devote more time to your maid than to her.

- Well let me put it this way. I go to mass every Sunday. I pay my dues to the Church. My wife makes generous donations to the poor. And you criticize me.

- Your relation with Lourdes sets a bad example!

- Well, well, bad example, eh?

Don Jâo got up, filled both cups with more wine, and asked the priest to come to the window. Raising their heads, the men surveyed the fields. They looked at the enslaved people laboriously engaged in their duties.

- Take a good look, Father. All of them have been baptized. Do they seem like people following bad examples? In my Hacienda, the maximum punishment is fifty lashes, and only in extreme cases. Cases like Quaky's. That brute set fire to my property and ran away. Now, arson is a bad example, isn´t it? So when I caught him I ordered fifty lashes. My wife and I are godparents to almost all the eldest children of our house hands. Not one of my slaves can claim that he has been mutilated in this Hacienda.

The priest tried to stop him. No doubt he was very far away from the point. But Don Jâo was in his own frenzy. The words came out like the roar of a tempestuous sea, wave after wave, violently.

- Yes, all of that is true, but...
- I have placed in service more blacksmiths, shoemakers, dyers, carpenters, than any other slave master in this region.
- Listen to me Don Jâo. Pay attention. I am talking about Lourdes and your wife.
- To be frank, Father, my wife is a lady; a very elegant and refined Portuguese lady. But look at that girl over there. Look at her thighs.
- Don Jâo, for God's sake, you are going too far.
- Look at the girl, Father. Look at her color. My wife is so damn white. Tomb white. But the Mulattas, just look at them.

Led by the priest, both men went back to there seats. Little Antonio ordered more wine and cheese and salted fish. He was curious to see what argument the priest could find to put Don Jâo in his place. But he knew it was a very hard one.

- It is not enough for Caesar's wife to be honest. She must also behave like an honest woman.

Father Elías seemed to be getting back his control of the situation.

- You have brought your own children to baptism...You are the godfather of your own children. Lourdes' children.
- Father —Don Jâo said cynically. Lourdiña is a married woman. Please respect her.
- I am no fool. Her husband is Black. But her children are too white to be the sons of a preto-retinto African.

LittleAntonio was amused but he could not smile. The protocol was very clear: he should not even hear the conversation. He could only stand at the door, waiting to be called, waiting, as it were, to be given the honor to serve.

- With all due respect, we are creating a new race, a cosmic race.

- Only God can create races- the priest snapped back fiercely –only God!

- All right then. God is using us to create a new race. In five generations we will all be Mulattos. All of us. The ruling class will be Mulatto. Brazil will be Mulatto.

Father Elías stood up.

- I think I am leaving. I promised your wife to speak to you about your relationship with your maid, and I have done so. I leave the matter to your conscience. Now I am on my way.

- Come on, Father. La Mandina is not going to beat you if you don't make it home in time for dinner. I expect the Governor and the Port Captain to come over at any moment.

Little Antonio could not help himself this time. He had to bite his lips to contain laughter. Among the enslaved the rumor was that the priest had intimate relations with La Mandina, a Black woman who served him loyally. Don Jâo was insidious.

- Please do me the honor and stay for the meeting. It's aboutPalmares.

The name, like a spell, made Father Elías reconsider his decision.

- Your wine is very good, Don Jâo.

Don Jâo laughed.

- Have some more. I'll see what I can do about the Lourdiña matter, Father. The flesh is weak, but I'll remember your sentence about Caesar's wife. I guess I need to be more discrete.

- What you need to do is to remember that you are a married man. A respectable Christian husband and father.

Someone people look up to, both free and slave. That is what you should remember.

Little Antonio's attention was no longer centered on the domestic conflict. He was no longer amused. Now he was concerned. A meeting of the Governor, the Port Captain and Don Jâo about Palmares meant trouble.

- Palmares!

The priest sighed.

- I was convinced that after the agreement with Ganga Zumba, we had achieved piece.

- Ganga is a genuine leader. He is truly concerned about his people. And we would have had peace if it was not for Juan Bautista and your beloved Francisco Zumbi.

- He is not my beloved.

- Now that is a very serious thing to say. Your predecessor trained him, taught him letters. Juan Bautista was already a corrupted Yayah when they brought him here, but the Church created both of these damn freaks. Can you imagine? Theology. Portuguese. For heaven's sake, Latin! Out of all subjects, Latin! I don't know, Father, but sometimes the Church…

- It was not the Church –Father Elias replied firmly –that wasFather Gonzalves's personal mistake.

- Yes of course. So you don't accept the responsibility. You created these monsters, and now you won't accept the responsibility.

Little Antonio could not listen to the priest's defense. One of the house hands came to tell him that the Governor was at the gate.

- Don Jâo, his Excellency the Governor is at the door.

- Great, let him in. And, by the way, tell the Señora that we have an extra guest: our Parochial Pastor. I am sure she will be delighted to attend to him.

Little Antonio went promptly to the door. He took another look at the mirror to make sure his presentation was adequate. He met the Governor and the Port Captain at the porch, and bowed to them with due respect, exactly as he was taught.

- Oh, ah… Little Antonio - the governor saluted him - always faithful. How is your mother?

Little Antonio's mother had died long before the Governor came to his city. In any case, the answer was not important. So he just murmured something between his teeth, and that was enough for his Excellency.

- Well, say hello to her for me -the Governor completed the salutation formula that he had devised whenever he faced house slaves. Especially in this case, since he was acquainted with the household.

Little Antonio escorted his Excellency to the library, and left immediately to tell the Señora how many guests she had. He rushed back to the kitchen and ordered them to change the cups and decanters. He then served more wine, dried fruits, salted fish and cheese. And, as was expected of him, he went back to the door and stood still, in a very awkward position, which according to the Señora was correct and elegant.

The conversation was now well advanced.

- Palmares is a blemish on my career. I have criticized the former Governors for not being able to cope with the problem, and I was so happy about the agreement with Ganga Zumba. But now, this restless Francisco Zumbi is acting as a cunning beast. I don't know what went wrong: he is supposed to be the educated one.

- He is under the influence of Juan Bautista, that Yayah devil – the priest seemed to justify –he goes around preaching in the name of Jesus, the imposter. The ignorant prietos worship him as a saint. And that little devil knows how to maintain his image, with his white woolly hair and beard.

- If you dress up the monkey in silk, that doesn't make a man out of him –the Port Captain complained bitterly.

- Well, a lot of slaves are now running away to Palmares, or as they call it, The Free Republic of Palmares.

The men laughed. There was a combination of scorn and forced admiration in that laughter. Zumbi meant hate. Zumbi meant dread. Zumbi meant secret admiration for his outstanding military victories which even the Port Captain who hated him so deeply had to acknowledge.

- Well you may call them monkeys if you want to – Don Jâo commented –but let me tell you this. When my father brought me to this country I was just a boy, but I can remember when he used to take part in the raids against the quilombeiros. Now, I am talking about ancient history; it has been a very long time since then.

- Monkeys –the Port Captain said with scorn. There are some astute monkeys around.

- So, if Zumbi is a monkey and we are men, and we can't get him, what does that say about us?

The Governor looked at the Port Captain harshly. The official could not afford an argument with Don Jâo. He was one of the most influential hacendados in the region, and a very rich man. He needed his support.

- We have to stop him! –he yelled, and standing up, went over to the window, hit the frame fiercely with his fist and turned to the men.

Little Antonio was getting very nervous. There was no way that the Governor was going to spend the rest of his life shouting and pounding on the frame. He felt relieved when Don Jâo asked what was on his mind.

- I have a plan.

The men drank from their cups. The Port Captain, in his effort to regain the ground he had lost in the discussion, proposed a toast to the Governor's idea. The men toasted, and again drank generously.

- I spoke to Domingos.

Little Antonio was shocked. Domingos Jorge Velho was a legend. They called him the "Indian hunter." He was famous for tracking down and killing Native people.

- And?

Father Elias too seemed carried away by the Governor's brilliant idea.

- We came to an agreement. He is willing to support us.

- Your Excellency –Father Elias said –your memories will live long after you.

The rest of the evening went by vaguely. Little Antonio could not concentrate on his job. His heart kept pounding wildly. He had to go through it all, the courtesies of the gentlemen in the presence of the women, including "my lovely and loving wife", "my beloved daughter", the food, the toasts, the merriment and – the greatest touch of cynicism of all –"my dear mother-in-law".

It was very late when the guests finally left. As expected, no one bothered to say goodbye to Little Antonio.

It was almost midnight when he made his way to Felicio's home.

- Felicio, take this money to Negra Lumbala. She will be very happy to see you. She says you are quite a man.

Felicio was very happy to hear Little Antonio's comment.

- Well, hurry on. You take the money and the letter to Negra. I am explaining to her that you desire to spend some time with her. Is that what you wanted me to write?

- Yes, thank you. Me cud tell her me self, but she like when man write her. Every time a tek a letta to her and the money you pay me fo gossip, she mek me spend a good, good, good time. The other night me no go wi letta. She tek the money and almost kick me outta the place. She se she too tired. But when me tek the letter, every thing is different."

- Make it back before dawn.

- Yes, yes, me will, me will…

Little Antonio went directly home. He told his wife about what he heard at the big house.

- You should not do anything about it. You have a good job. If Don Jâo catches any of your letters, you will be a dead man. And what about the children? You seem to have no consideration for the children.

Little Antonio went over to the children's bunks. A couple of angels, they were. He caressed his daughter's head for a while, and then went over to the other bunk, sat beside his son and held his hand.

Later, he could not sleep and it was almost four when he heard some sort of commotion outside. His wife leaped from her bunk and ran to the door. She slipped out quietly and a few moments later came back with the news.

- I told you this was going to happen. They caught Felicio on his way back. What are you going to do now?

- Nothing, woman. Nothing. Calm down. Let me handle this. Little Antonio changed clothes and walked over to the big house. There was Felicio, tied by the neck, standing in a hanging position. He was almost on the tip of his toes. Don Jâo was totally outraged, but Felicio hung on to the truth.

- Mi spen de night at Negra Lumbala house. Please believe me. Me spen de night at Negra Lumbala. Don Jâo that is all me du. Me spen night at Negra Lumbala. Sir... please, sir, please, Me spen night at Negra Lumbala. Me spen night at Negra Lumbala. Me spen night at Negra Lumbala. Me spen night at Negra Lumbala...

Felicio was telling the truth. But his humble begging tone was irritating. Little Antonio came as close as he could to Don Jâo.

- Señor —he said at the very first opportunity he had —do you want me to find out if he is telling the truth? I can find out with Negra Lumbala herself. She will trust me.

Don Jâo seemed to calm down a little.

- All right.

He turned to the overseer.

- Let Little Antonio find out. Give Felicio twenty-five lashes for leaving the Hacienda without permission. Twenty-five lashes right now, and keep him tied till mid day. If what he says is true, let him go. If he is lying, give him another ten lashes, and another ten, and another ten, until he tells the truth. Keep me informed. God, what a burden for us White men! One can not even get a good night's sleep.

Little Antonio saved Felicio from further grief. Then he settled down to work very hard. He had been very lucky up to the moment, but that was close. Too close. Yet at the same time, he knew that his position was key to the movement, and could not bring himself to abandon what he considered his duty.

His wife was right, no doubt about that. He had a good job. Although a slave like all others, being in a position of authority in the big house gave him a certain advantage. Also, both Don Jâo and his wife trusted him.

He had sense this preferential treatment since childhood. He could remember many instances in which Don Jâo, then a young man, would call him and give him a fruit or some sweet. Sometimes he wondered why. His mom hated the young Jâo and tried hard to pretend she did not see his inclination to pet Antonio. There was another consideration to add. Little Antonio's skin was lighter than that of his brothers. That caused him many problems, especially from one of the children, who gave him the nickname "Red Ebo." And he hated him for that. The name set him aside, put him on the outskirts of the group.

It was Zumbi, now the head of the Palmares Free Republic, who explained to him his personal history. While living with the former Rector, they had become close friends. Francisco, as his White masters called him, was a very good student, and wanted to become a priest. He applied himself with all his might to the teachings he got from Father

Gonzalves, and learned to read and write, and taught Little Antonio. One day Little Antonio raised the matter of color to Francisco. He wondered why, in his own family, he felt discrimination. The point was that he was much whiter than the others were. Francisco, who was becoming very harsh about White people, sort of suggested the well-kept secret.

- You should ask your mother. Tell her to explain what happened with this damn Jâo.

- You mean Don Jâo? She doesn't like him. Well, actually she hates him.

- She has a very good reason to hate him.

- But… what does that have to do with the color of my… No! It can't be!

Little Antonio did ask his mother about the color of his skin. She said that God created people according to His will, and that in this case he had some sort of mission for Little Antonio that he could only fulfill if he was a light-skinned Mulatto. He was just born that way –she said –and he should use his advantage to benefit the family.

Little Antonio was not satisfied, so he asked her why she hated Don Jâo. The question placed in the context of the conversation, infuriated and then embarrassed his mother. She reacted violently and slapped him on his mouth.

- Never say that again! Do you have any appreciation for your mother? What do you want? You want them to give me fifty lashes and then sell me to another farm; that's what you want, eh? You want to get rid of me? I should have known that no good would come out of you, and strangle you when you were a baby.

She went into a fit, and cried and acted like someone possessed by some evil spirit. For days she did not even say "good morning" to Little Antonio. But on Sunday after mass she told him to accompany her to her favorite tree. She murmured some sort of ceremonial words Little Antonio could not understand. She took shrub and used it to sprinkle water on Antonio, and spilled some liquor at the root of the tree. She then embraced Little Antonio, and told him in a very humble tone how much she loved him. And she asked him never to say again that she hated Don Jâo because he was her master, and could dispose of her very easily, by just sending her away. "You are the rightful descendent of Kuama, a believer in the Spirit. Aba and Kuama are the builders. The Orishas. You come directly from them. Nothing else matters. You are a Yamba person.

- A what?
- A Yamba person.

She then embraced him, putting foreheads together, rubbing their noses, reassuring him that she was so glad that she had not strangled him when he was a baby, that she thanked God for that.

Little Antonio went to see Francisco and told him about the strange conduct of his mother, and asked who Kuama was and what in the world was a Yamba person.

Francisco listened to him for a while, and then said solemnly:

- She meant a Yayah person. And the name is Kwami. According to the traditions of the elders, Kwame and Aba are the king and queen of the Yayah Kingdom. You should not be hard on your mother. She was then very young. What I heard from Old Mambo before he died is that Jâo forced her over and over again. She was afraid of being sold to another farm, and not being able to see her family any more. So she had to submit. Then one day Jâo's father found them together. He whipped her and sent her family to do field work.

Francisco walked to the window.

- You know, you have been well treated. This I must admit. At least, the beast finally has some sort of consideration for his child.

- I am not his child. I know who my father is. I am a
Yamba person. Ganga Zumba is my father. He is father to all
of us.

When Francisco found out that because of his color he
could not become a priest he became a very radical opponent
to the system. It was then that he began his association with
Juan Bautista, who lead him to Zumba. Later, he decided to
escape and become a citizen of Palmares and then change his
name to Zumbi. Antonio thought of Ganga Zumba, who his
friend so mystically depicted as an African God, and about
Juan Bautista, who the slaves look up to as an Orisha and a
prophet. Francisco asked Little Antonio to go with him, but
he did not.

Yes, his wife was right. He had a good job in the big
house. Although enslaved like all the others, he was trusted by
both Don Jâo and his wife. But most important to him was
his sense of loyalty to Zumbi's cause.

So he held his ground.

On Sunday Domingos came to see Don Jâo. He was
a strange character, indeed a legend. He was wearing the
famous necklace, made of the ears of the native chiefs that he
had killed. He came with his bodyguards, a savage looking
and stinking mob. There were five of them; three White
men, an Indian servant and an enslaved Black male. The
bodyguards did not exactly reflect the composition of his
private army, since according to Little Antonio's information
he commanded one hundred Whites, a few Blacks, a
thousand Indian men, plus the women and children. They
were a nomad- like mob, paid by the Hacendados of Recife
to "clear" the land from the infection of the "primitive" tribes.
He specialized in suppressing Indian rebellions, and boasted
about his heroic deeds. He wore the necklace as proof of his
achievement, and was proudly responsible for the death of
tens of thousands of Indians.

He was now a person of a certain age, and was finally seeking a place to settle down with his mob. Little Antonio overheard some of the petitions: four positions for his people in the three religious orders of Portugal; he would retain all the Blacks that he captured in the raid on Palmares as his own slaves; he wanted a free supply of arms, munitions and food.

Little Antonio did not hear the other conditions. But that evening he wrote the usual letter to inform Zumbi about the danger. Nine thousand white men, Indians and Mulattos would be marching against Palmares.

Felicio was not very happy about the errand, but the temptation to be with Negra Lumbala was a better beacon to survival than his fear. Those were the only true moments of happiness in his "damn life". That was what he said, and he would risk his life for them.

But this time, Felicio was captured on his way to Negra Lumbala's house. The sentinels alerted her on time, and she escaped, but the valuable information they were sending to Zumbi was now in the hands of Don Jâo. It was true that don Jâo had no clue that Little Antonio could write, but he would soon find out, whether by deduction or by Felicio's confession. Little Antonio knew it was the end of his career as an informant. He went over to the children's bunk, and kissed them tenderly. He rubbed their forehead and nose against his. Then he hugged his wife, who said nothing. She just cried silently.

- Go to the Señora. Tell her that I was forced to write a letter to Zumbi, and then kidnapped by the Maroons from Palmares. Make a big fuss. Cut yourself or something, tear up your cloths, mash up the house, and start shouting from here. All I need is a few minutes. She will help you. Take good care of the children. I'll send for you as soon as I can —then he was gone.

NAT

This is the dawn of the Day of the Lord. And the Lord has said from this moment on "I hand Sihon over to thee, the people and the land. You may now enter his territory and seize everything thing you find in his country."

NAT sat on the mound, his eyes wide open, taking into his lungs the fresh Virginia air, watching the days and nights, as the year 1831 went by in turmoil. They were at that sacred spot in the center of time, a selected group they were, chosen as disciples. They were the special few, the Children of Israel.

They had had a good night, a real banquet included, with the very best of everything. The house slaves had done a good job, smuggling out the food used only in the master's kitchen. But Nat himself did not eat. He fasted for them all.

After the meal he called to Madison, his favorite disciple, asked him to hold the Bible and summoned the men to the mound. Beside them, Big Job stood, towering. It was he who requested silence.

- Let us listen to the Word of Our Lord —Big Job said —as revealed to our brother Nat, his Apostle.

- Brethren, the hour has arrived.

A deep silence came into the camp, forcing attention on them. They were all in one vibration now, all in one spirit, all in one purpose, and all in one unspoken promise to live or to die.

- These are the words of the Lord written in this Book I was told to read to you today. So pay close attention.

Nat then opened the Bible, randomly, so that they could all see. He did not chose the page as the White Pastor did at the White church while Big Job stayed some distance away and tended to the horses. Nat was a different kind of Pastor, he seemed to have the ancestral solemnity he used to admire in his uncle when he was a boy. Nat just opened the book and began to read.

- The Lord told me, from this moment I give thee —now, pay attention to this, I give thee Sihon. Who is Sihon? Sihon is the king of Heshbonites. All the Whites of this district are Heshbonites. They are the grandchildren of King Sihon, so, Brethren, pay attention to this: I have opened the Bible and have said to the Lord, Lord, let my eyes fall on the Word that you want me to deliver this day. And as you see, brother Job is my witness. I have called to Madison my brother, I have told him to hold the Bible and I have opened on the page that the Lord indicated and here are His words. You all saw what I did. So there can be no doubt in your hearts. Here is the Word of God, so Brethren, shout Hallelujah!

- Hallelujah, praise the Lord —they said

- This is the dawn of the Day of the Lord. And the Lord has said from this moment on "I hand Sihon over to thee, the people and the land. You may now enter his territory and seize everything thing you find in his country."

- Hallelujah. Glory to God. Glory to God that speaks to us.

- When the Children of Israel heard those words of the Lord, they destroyed the cities of the Heshbonites and they killed all — men, women and children, as was the Will of the Lord. And they only spared the life of the animals and kept the things of value from his enemies. Glory to the Lord. I am reading here from this book of Deu...to Deu... to...ronomy... Deuteronomy, Nat said, and Madison also drooped before the Bible when he saw his leader reading from his master's favorite book. How could that be? The same book, how could such different words coming from the same source mean such opposite things? But Nat read and the men said, "Glory, hallelujah to the Lord." The men said they would follow Nat's instructions, for evidently it was the Will of the Lord God. It was there, they had heard.

- Now, Nat continued with a firm voice –it doesn't say tomorrow.

The followers then said "Amen" and Nat went on with his sermon.

- Yes, hallelujah, the Word says starting from this moment, and this moment is tonight. Amen, glory to the Lord that has revealed his Word to us –he said emphatically –and Big Job shouted "you heard the Brother, so say Amen", and they all said "Amen" but Big Job could not hear them, so he demanded another and another and yet another Amen, until he got it right. Madison then closed the book and placed it on a rock, and the great silence came back.

The teachings of his grandmother returned to him that night. While fasting –and he fasted for forty days and nights –he saw her on the ship. He was sitting at her knee as in a dream, listening to her and she was on the ship.

But then he was carried away, as by the Spirit of the Lord, and was no longer in his grandmother's lap but rather in her head. And through her eyes he could see the dark and cold cabin. He perceived her confusion in that dark and frightening cabin, the body just beside her. He saw her fighting again to take off the enormous body, using both hands. She held her breath in order to avoid the offensive stench coming from the mouth of the body. The eyes of the body were red. And from her eyes tears shed copiously as she tried in vain to rotate her head, so the tears would not mix with the flow coming from the nose of a stranger. For the first time in her life, she could perceive the scent of earwax. The body became dense. It was already touchable. She wanted to move her own body, to move herself away, but there was no response, except for the paralyzing effect of horror.

And Nat understood then that bodies sweat, that they produce gases that they burp, that they expel the remnants of food and drink, and bodies like his grandmother's obey the monthly cycle of life. And at that very moment he understood what it was be a woman, with that lukewarm liquid running from her naked legs, and Nat could not bear the smell. He could not believe that that body was his grandmother's body, because he remembered her tenderness, he remembered her fragrance, the smell of wild herbs and mint. He wanted to get out of her head, but he was not able to. He felt the agony of captivity, stronger than the one he had experienced personally, the force of decay in her body, in our body. Because her body was our own body profaned. And bodies sweat. And bodies menstruate. And bodies fart.

But then, he felt grandmother's warm hands caressing his head.

- My lucky sleeping boy, she said, but you should not sleep, because you are called to be the liberator, because you are J. B. C's grandson.

One day, his mother, playing with his name, discovered that J. B. C. were the initials of John Baptist Congo, direct descendant of the Yayahs, who using the power of the prophets, managed to open the channels of knowledge for his town. It was interesting that, when the grandmother pronounced those initials, it was as though they had a magic effect, and the boy dozed again and saw the day of rebellion. He listened to the shouting and screaming of women on the ship's deck; he saw the convulsing desperation that even the cooks stopped to watch, wondering what strange spell had taken possession of the Africans while fearing for their lives.

Now, on the stone, he had read the Word of God.

- First —Nat said —we have to act like the old Israelis. That is the Lord's way. And then later, once we are strong enough to have our own army, once we can match the Heshbonites, we will then allow the women and the children to live, and they will be our women and our children, so is the Will of the Lord. But at dawn, leave no man or woman or child alive.

Many, many years ago the grandmother was at the bank of the river, fishing. She was no longer a young woman. She had a few years on her body, but not the hands of men. In fact, the last man to touch her had been the Captain of the slave ship. It was that touch that moved her into a position to help the leader capture the ship and liberate the slaves.

She heard a flock of dogs coming her way, so she pulled up her raft and hid herself under the trees, dodging with her arch and arrow and an old rifle that she always kept loaded, prepared for flight down the river or for personal defense.

As she waited for the unpredictable outcome, she saw a tall, rather cadaverous man, with features very similar to those she knew too well in her distant hometown. Without counting the risk, she threw herself off the raft, and making her way to the bank she dragged him as she could. Mounting the fugitive on the raft from his waist up, she began to make her escape.

From a distance, she listened to the dogs barking at the river bank and the voices of the hunters trying to make them cross the current, in order to look for the footprints of the fugitive on the other side of the river and continue the chase. She simply kept her pace, as quickly as she could, until she saw the watchman's tree where she knew there would be guards that would send out the alarm, and that others would certainly be waiting further downstream. She signaled twice, as she should, and sat down on her raft to wait for the outcome of that unexpected episode.

Once in the camp, she told them the man she rescued was a Yayah, therefore, her relative.

Days came and went. She looked after him and fed him devotedly, curing his wounds until he regained consciousness. He said his name was J.B.C, son of a famous warrior and a Christian. So Nat's grandmother, after feeding him and lovingly restoring him to health, decided that he was the most handsome man she had ever seen. She also thought him good enough for her to submit to a strange ceremony the Christians call Baptism, and later to accept a Christian marriage. And she swore by the name of He who her husband insisted was the true God. She then committed herself to the sole idea to live the rest of her days in peace. She told every one that, through this total and non submissive passion, it was her chance to erase the bad memory of the bodies that sweat and stink, of the bodies that smell like liquor, of the irreverent hands of a so called doctor that she heard saying "cheeskleen" or something of the sort, and although because of her age she couldn't count on children, she was so happy to have finally found the man of her dreams. He reminded her of Papah Kwame.

Nat's mother was a total surprise. She was the child of old age, a sign according to J.B.C., that the Lord had a specific plan for her life. She was consecrated to the Ancestors according the Yayah tradition, and blessed by the Pastor of his clandestine Church of the Holy Stream. For the ceremony, they had to travel a good distance, coming closer than she had ever been to the plantations.

It was there that she listened to the words of the Bible for the first time. The Pastor explained that when God created the human being, he created them male and female. It was there that she was told, much to her disgust, that she was now to become the daughter of a Mister Abraham and no longer a member of Elder Kwame's clan. But her love for J.B.C. was so strong that she endured it all, not allowing herself to leap up in rebellion and shout the big question.

- Is that Captain that raped me also a son of Abraham? Is the White cook that tossed hot oil into my cousin's eyes "because him was staring at me, Captain –said the Cook –and him had no right to stare on a White man, you know?" – Is he also a son of Abraham? Are the savage slave hunters with their dogs, those that were coming after you, my beloved J.B.C., are they also children of Abraham? How come we are becoming members of the Abraham family?

J.B.C. told her that there was a difference between the teachings of the Church and its members. He said that the Bible, the mysterious book that only the Pastor could read, contained such truths as the fundamental idea of a God that was One and Three. She remembered the words of the old wise man explaining to them that there was only one God, and that was an Egyptian idea, that He has Three Persons. It was the same old song the Griot sang, about Nyame, the Creator, manifested as Odomankoma, Asase Yaa and Kwaku Anansi, except that in this case, the Second Identity of the Goodhead was female. The same story told by a young boy named Juan Bautista, who daring to speak to the Elders without their permission, explained that in this new land Egypt was the Symbol of Evil, and that God's new name was Jehovah, and that the holy names of the Divine Trinity were no longer Ra, Osiris, and Iris, but Father, Jesus and the Holy Spirit.

But if there is only one God (she did not rebel or questioned her husband), then it is that same God that gave the Black Man the will to resist. It would have been He who inspired in the Yayahs and the Sumani and in all the rest of them, their vocation to hold on to the Samamfo –the community of ancestors, living and unborn –the stamina and the conviction to connect themselves to the very essence of life, to go deep beyond suffering, to revisit the Source and sing His tunes; yes, if there was only One God, not only one almighty God, but just one God, then it was He that gave them the vitality to prolong the ceremony way into the morning.

But while they congregated to pray, and to wish the best for J.B.C.'s family, they were attacked by White guards, who claimed to be the children of Abraham, and although her husband prayed so hard, invoking God's help, he was captured, and she was taken prisoner again, and there she was, the ugly memories of the ship haunting her, holding her daughter, remembering how, back in the land of the Yayahs when the Fulahghi attacked, mothers fought desperately to at least keep their children together.

Memories, yes, bitter, painful, the ship again, again the ship, holding on to her daughter, taken away from her husband, her lawful husband, her Christian husband, in the name of the God of Abraham who they all declared as God, slaves and masters in such perfect communion, loving their brothers as they love themselves.

This time, the people on the ship spoke another language, but all the rest was the same, including the cross and the hutch for the women. She clung on to her daughter, holding her tight to her chest, as they were sold to another master, she and her daughter, holding on if not for happiness at least to be a family, to be able to talk about J.B.C. Holding on together and praying that by the grace of God and the help of the Ancestors, she would be able to raise her daughter.

And so she did. She never saw J.B.C. again, but she lived on. Her daughter caught on to the new language, and secretly, while playing with the White kids, learned how to read. It was she who explained to her mother that J.B.C. was in fact John Baptist Congo, just another way to say Juan Bautista Congo, who had changed his name for some reason or the other, maybe to accommodate to the spirit of the new language. She did nothing to suppress her daughter's fantasy. J.B.C. was a great man, who tried to find freedom through religion, who thought that if he became part of the Christian community he would be respected as a person.

In time, the old lady took on the legend all by herself, and told Nat's mother that her son was the Messenger. So Nat was appointed and reared by his grandmother as the Elected, the Heir of the Yayah tradition, the Great Messenger consecrated by God in order to liberate the Black slaves of the region.

Nat stood up on the mound. Nat stood up in faith, a faith that was immense, much bigger than Big Job, firmer than

Madison's will. Many of his followers would remember him like that at the moment of death, his brilliant illuminated face in the light of the bonfire, standing, facing the same Supreme God for whose cause his ancestors died, facing Jehovah, the God of vengeance, the God of the armies, the Jealous God, the God that became man to accomplish the liberation of man, of humankind, on this Day of Redemption. Nat said, standing on the mound, "we are the Children of Israel." Many would remember him just like that, a prophetic resonance, like the announcement of the never-ending struggle to be, as the force from the Samamfo. And night became more night when the attack began.

They went directly toward the Big White House: Nat, Hark, Big Job, Nelson, Sam, Will, Henry and Madison.

Joseph Travis, the one that made them call him master, had a reputation of being a cruel slave master. He sat on his bed in the middle of drowsiness caused by the bad whiskey he drank the night before, trying to figure out where the strange noises were coming from. Hark and Nat used a ladder to get up to the top of the house and lowered themselves through the chimney and were able to enter the Big House without being detected. They took possession of the firearms and Nat and Will went to Travis'room. The slave master now jumped from his bed, trying desperately to save his life, calling to his wife. But Will leveled him with a single blow from his axe.

Miss Travis, as the wife was called, panicked and began to scream, but she was silenced with another mortal blow. The same fate was dealt to the children. But one of the loyal slaves, called Jim, was spending the night in the Big House with one of the slaves. Alarmed at seeing so many dead bodies of men, women and children piled in the patio, Jim ran to warn his half-brother Harris about the rebellion. Harris managed to escape on time, seeking help in the neighboring districts to put down the uprising.

Jim thus saved the life of his White half brother, but then, when the rulers recovered control and began to hunt down the now fugitive Blacks he refused to help in the hunt.

- Me save you life —he told his brother —but sah, me not able to help you kill off my people, sah, after all, sah, all them want is freedom, so, sah, jus, jus put you gun here, aim here at me heart and help me out of this pain —and his half brother did exactly so, he pointed his gun, aiming directly at the heart, and without hesitation or a word sent Jim off to give account of his deeds to the Lord.

Madison fled to save his life. Behind him he left his wife, the woman whom he loved. He fled, but as he fled he swore to return to rescue her.

Fifty-five white cadavers lay in the patio at morning. Seventy-three Black cadavers. But all of them had bled in red.

MADISON

Night is cold. The moon
beckoned to him with a whitish
glow, as the wild sounds of the
wind caused the fugitive's
heart to pound against his
chest.

MADISON kept himself hidden in the swamp until he was convinced that they would be looking for him further away. Then, bitten by insects and tortured by hunger, he began his slow road to liberty. Left behind was the woman he loved. They both truly loved each other and were prepared to fight to be together. She was a Mulatto, the daughter of the owner of the plantation, and of the adopted grandmother who reared Madison.

Night is cold. The moon beckoned to him with a whitish glow, as the wild sounds of the wind caused the fugitive's heart to pound against his chest. With a small knife as his only weapon, he succeeded in procuring his dinner by killing a dog that attacked him. Raw meat and blood to keep life in his body, but at the same time, those were a painful remembrance of death lying everywhere in his home town. And the ugly image of Nat captured, tortured, confessing names of the living and the dead, and the so called "Heshbonite" survivors celebrating with blood their vengeance, stepping over the Black cadavers over and over again, as if two hundred years of assault, rape and oppression in the name of God had not been enough.

Madison could also remember standing in the churchyard, hearing the eco of the pastors' sermons, which made it clear to all that God had elected the White man as his people, and given them the responsibility of bring civilization to the rest of mankind. And he could also recall overhearing the pastor explaining to his son that when a people –White People –accepted the Peace of The Lord, they were entitled, as a reward for bringing the rest of mankind closer to God, to have the benefit of those people's labor while they were being taught to work. That is the Will of the Lord, written in the Book of Deuteronomy, the very same book from which Nat drew his conclusion that the time had come for redemption. A very, very strange book it was. How could the same words taken from the same book contain messages of liberation and oppression at the same time?

Madison continued on his way, close to the road, advancing as fast as he could. He was caught between the satisfied hunger and nausea, with pain coming from his wounded foot.

Two nights later he succeeded crossing the state border. He did not know it however, so he just continued North. But by the third night he could not go on any more. So he simply gave way, loosing blood, thinking about the soft brook in which he used to bath whenever he could escape from his mother and his master.

He woke up in a barn, attended by two White women. He tried to get up, caught by panic, expecting some sort of torture. But the women signaled for him to be quiet. There was something about them that made him feel that the war was over. So he let his head rest on the pillow and almost instantly went back to sleep.

From there on, the freedom flight was easier. He traveled for many nights and days, helped by Mulattos, Whites and Blacks, without understanding why they were all caring, feeding and helping him in every possible way, instead of capturing and returning him to "his master." About a week after that they told him that he was on his way to Canada.

He finally did get to Canada. He was employed on a farm, and for the first time in his life he got paid for his work.

His employer was very happy with his services and rewarded him with plenty of food and a good shelter.

It was not long before Madison recovered his impressive strength and forgot about the dog's meat and blood that saved his life. But he could not forget his wife. He spent much of his spare time thinking about her, until he could take no more. He then confronted his employer about his decision, and after some harsh discussion, managed to hit the road again.

He went back the same way, but this time, he had a document declaring him free, document that proved its worth in some states and places.

Back home, he succeeded in seeing his wife, and they planned to escape. But someone told his wife's half-brother, who was now the head of the plantation, that they had seen Madison around.

After the older Travis died during the rebellion, young Master Travis, his son, who survived miraculously, had taken over. He made a major effort and captured Madison. He also accused his half-sister of complicity, and sold them both to different slave- traders.

Suddenly it was night in Madison's life. At least during the days in Canada he knew where to find his wife. But now his dreams had been shattered, and his only consolation was to think that from now on he could be in total rebellion, since life had no meaning without his wife. He was taken away chained and humiliated. His fame as a brave and very strong man was of concern, especially since among the Blacks there was rumor that he had made his way to Canada and back, all by himself.

Now that he had lost his wife, Madison had no more time to lose. He was prepared to offer his life for the cause of liberty, which he considered a substantial part of being human. He had been out of slavery. He had lived in a completely different society and had had a taste of good will.

This time he would not run. So he started to talk to fellow slaves about Nat's ideas and his word fell on fertile ground.

On the fourth day aboard the slave ship, on his way to the Caribbean, they were caught up in a hurricane. The wind gave both captors and captives a very hard time. The Captain ordered the women to come up on the deck. One of the guards, taking advantage of the confusion forced one of the women into a corner, hoping to rape her, but she managed to hit him fatally, and got hold of the keys. None of the guards found out what had happened. It was thought that the dead body was the result of the confrontation with nature, and since the danger was on-going, no one had any idea about the keys being in the hands of the slaves.

Next morning, with the calm of the new day, came mutiny, lead by Madison. He managed to capture all of the White crew, killing only one, and he offered them their lives if they sailed the ship to a British Port. The agreement was kept and the ship and slaves got safely into Port Nassau.

But for Madison, there was an extraordinary compensation to his efforts. His wife was among the women on board.

CUDJOE

- Now open you eyes. Remember we don't bukunu –we don't kneel down to nobody.

EDDY had his own story.

When the horn blew, he jumped. He had a nervous character, which made a very good sentinel out of him. The men looked at each other, held their guns and rose from their seats. Eddy turned to Cudjoe, the leader of this Jamaican Maroon freedom fighter squadron with respect and said:

- Me going bring him to you –Cudjoe nodded.

- All right –and to the other men:

- Now open you eyes. Remember we don't bukunu –we don't kneel down to nobody.

After a while, Eddy came back escorting a strange looking man. His hair was blue-black and straight; pointed nose; dark bronze skin. But his body had the build of a Mandingo.

- Well I be damn, who dis?-

- Him is Jamaican.

- So what kind of foolishness is dat? All a we ah Jamaican.

- Yes, but him is from this very Land of the Springs. Yu know that that is what Jamaica means. Him mother a Arawak Indian. Him father Black.

- So if the man is a damn Miskito Indian why you don't shoot him?

- Him want to talk, man. Him father is African. Him not from Central America.

Cudjoe stepped down from the stone on which he had taken a position. A short, vigorous, and strongly built man, he wore a blue sleeveless riding coat that the Spaniards call "casaca". He had a wide band around his head that marked his authority. An old hat barely covered his rounded head. On his right side a horn full of gun powder, and a sack of pieces of metal used for bullets. Hanging under his left arm, was a machete in its leather sheath. His shirt and other clothing as well as his body were soiled with the reddish dirt of the barricades.

-But yu know that the Miskito are all allies of the British. Them come with them to Jamaica to help kill Maroons.

-Him is African by father and right here from Jamaica.

- This shit must be Blackshot, a damn traitor working for British.. And me feel is foolishness mek you bring him here. But any way, what is done is done. Whe you from?

- Jamaica.

Cudjoe laughed.

- Me too.

- No, I mean: native Jamaican. Me name Arrow Walk. Me mother was Arawak Indian and me father Clearvalley.

- No Black man name so. You want to mek a fool out o' me?.

- No sir. Well him real name was Carabalí. Maroon from Esmeraldas Valley. Am, somewhere in the Andes mountain them seh, near whe them have some place called Equator, or something like that. Only Africans live there. One day him fall asleep in the woods and the Spanish man them capture him and sell him as slave, and him master sell him to a man from Panama, and then him end up here on a Jamaican Plantation.

- So, then you is Miskito Indian.

Arrow Walk was offended.

- You hurt me man, you hurt me bad. Me is a Cottawood. We fighting for freedom just like yu. I swear to God. Me love roast pig, you know?

This time he sounded like a true Jamaican.

- So wha yu come here fo?

- Yu in danger. A ship off bay, with about two hundred sailors. And the Governor have bout the double, Blackshots, Miskito Indian, slaves and all that. Ah was working with Colonel Needham and ah use to pass information to Big Joe. Yu must know him. Big Joe, the Madagascar man. But them catch Big Joe and juk him and poke him and almost beat the life out of him. So before him tell on me, ah convince Needham that ah know you personally and that I could get you to sign a treaty. But that is not what me want to do. Ah come here to warn you and to fight fa freedom.

Cudjoe asked Eddy to step aside.

- Wha you bring him here fa? De man is a damn spy.

- No, no. Him want to fight. When him want, him can talk English just like you, and him can talk like the English them. And him can talk Spanish, you nevuh can tell if them ah coming back. Them rule this land befor, and them might come back. This man is free, him have papers.

- The English sen him to watch we. Him must be Blackshot, or Miskito Indian. You same one seh him talk Spanish.

- Him is a Cottawood man! The man love him roast pig you noh!

- All right, tell you what; bring, am, Jon and Done. If him work with Needham either him know them, or them will know him. If not, we no tek no chance.

A few minutes later, Jon and Done joined them. Jon was a lean, tall white boy, with blue eyes and blond hair. Done wasshort, reddish skin, reddish hair, with a strange sore on his lips. As they came into the cave, Jon went pale.

- What the hell that brute doing here? –he said, pointing to Arrow Walk. That is Needham's sitting stool, as Mr. Cudjoe like to say.

- Ah, look yah no? The two White pigs them. I remembah when Yu try to save youself an almost frig up everybody else.

Jon jumped toward Arrow Walk with the intention to hit him. But Walk was faster. The White lad seemed ridiculous hitting the breeze.

- Eddy, stop them!
- All right, you hear the man, cut it out! Cudjoe turned to Jon.
- So you know him?
- Yes; him a damn worthless Indian.

Cudjoe put an end to the meeting: he ordered them to giveWalk food and watch him. He then turned to Eddy:

- Tell you what; send him back to buy gun powdah. If what him seh is true, we have to get whole barril of gun powdah, and a big sack of shots. Tell Done to write letter to the Jew, what's him name?

- Jacob.

- All right, get Quashee Yayah to go with him. No, no, you go with him. Let him go on his own but watch him. Tell him we going move to um, Saint Elizabeth to join up with the Madagascars. Tell him that is a secret, so if him chat or them catch him, that is what him will tell them. Now, don't fool around: if the man try to play any Nancy trick on you just sen him home to him Arawak mother. Ask Sam Yayahson to take care of him, but tell him, him must careful. And find out more 'bout the White man them plans.

A week later Walk and Eddy were back safely. Sam Yayahson came with them. He had to run away because "them catch Gully and him tell them 'bout how we fool up the Church Street Jew, making him believe with the letter that the gunpowder is for Needham."

The new report confirmed Walk's information. Six hundred men, two hundred from the ship "Commodore", two hundred voluntary local Whites and two hundred Blackshot, Miskito Indian and carriers were coming after them.

Cudjoe laid out his plans carefully. Without naming his source he told his top officials about the attack that the

Whites were planning. And they organized the defense. One hundred men were placed at Crow Hill, and another hundred at Hobby Road. The women should take up the entire crop, and hide it in the small village on the other side of the Hill. If the Whites got near they should burn the village, take the children and run to the Guy.

That very evening a messenger came from the salt makers of Long Bay. Things were very serious this time. Both men had told them about the ship that they believed the English Majesty sent for. Next morning, spies from Port Antonio came rushing to tell Cudjoe that the governor knew exactly the location of the Maroons.

Early Thursday morning horns blew. The main body of the troop was coming directly to the crossing. It was obvious that they were pressing to get to the top because that would help them find the route. They went exactly where the Maroons wanted them, and were easily ambushed.

"So we fire on them from one side. And some of them fall down dead or half dead. And his Majesty's troop them turn to fire back on pure bush, you know, on the bush because after we fire we lay down stiff on we belly. Then we wait 'til them fire from the other side and lay down on them belly and we get up and fire again. So before the White man them know what to do fire broke out from the other side of the road, right behind them. So now you see them confounded. Them can't decide were to answer the fire: right or left. And to make them get real mad we start to fire from the front and them get wild and burst loose. Boy that was the first time ah see White man run like that. Them begin to throw away all that them was carrying and run. Ah mean every thing, you know: meat, medicine, bread, gun powder, and cannon bullet. All them carry with them was the liquor. We pin them down at Shaky Rock, and we was bound to kill all of them but the rain start pouring down all day and night and them run away. Them run in the dark and since it was not safe to run behind them we just let them run. Any way, we catch Murriah, the Blackshot and Cudjoe was happy 'bout that. Him was good hearted to people that fight for freedom but him hate traitors. Murriah was a brave Black soldier, no body can take that away from him. Him fight on the side of the Whites but the man was no coward. No coward at all. But him was a beast. Through him and the Miskito the Governor manage to find one of Cudjoe camp them, and almost blast us up, you know? Cudjoe had no mercy for that sort of a dirty bastard.

'We not cruel like the Whites, him tell him, so seh you prayers Murriah." Murriah was brave to death. All him do was to look at Cudjoe and laugh and scorn him:

- You savage Black animal.

Cudjoe look at him

- Wah color you are sah?'

- Yes, me Black too, but me no savage.

- But you go dead same way.

Cudjoe himself shot him and we left him body fo' the crows.

LADIES IN BED

Who is she, Jacques? Who is she? –a lance mutilating my body; a bullet in my wounds. Who is she, Jacques? ...- C'est ma femme –the traitor said, as he tried to greet me but I didn't answer...

GOD! I need you darling. Your voice. I love it when you say Mathildá, with your amusing Continental accent. God. You are a part of me, Jacques. Jacques, I am waiting. I am waiting to be yours forever. I have taken care of myself to be finally yours. And my expectations are not only mine. I could see the tension on the faces of my Octoroon parents. Both my father and my mother stood watching the ship dock.

It was as if yesterday when you went off to France to study. We cried like children, and made promises. Remember how we trembled? It is exactly the same tremor assaulting us now while we wait for the moment of reunion, and the opportunity to carry out our most precious dream.

Now, there you are... sun of my life. But, who is that horrible woman standing beside you? Who is she, Jacques? Who is she? –a lance mutilating my body; a bullet in my wounds. Who is she, Jacques? I can see my father advancing toward you, and hold me mom, hold me tight, I swear that I will faint if your loving hand does not give me the strength I need, mom, sustain me as usual, help me cling on to life. Who is she, Jacques? I can see him greeting my mom, and please don't use the words I am afraid you're going to...Who is she, Jacques?

- C'est ma femme –the traitor said, as he tried to greet me but I didn't answer... I could not respond in any event. I hated him.

Then we started moving solemnly down the road, away from the sea, followed by the trunk carriers. The town was watching, delighted with the idea that Jacques had returned to Saint Dominique. I could feel the glances of the girls, wondering about us. They were as surprised as I was about this unannounced French lady, ugly as she is, and they stared at my parents and at Jacques' family. Gradually I became aware that the town did not see us as separate families. For them we were a unit, an entity. But, awe, no longer! Now she is; not me. And she has divided us for ever.

Why, Jacques? My father is a White Mulatto, an Octoroon. He has administered the export-import business of your family and has done it well. He has been as good as any one could. He is a rich man. My mother is also almost white. Our family possesses a large country property. There is no reason to justify not marrying me. We know each other well. We have been raised together. And we have loved each other intensely since childhood. So, why, Jacques, why?

Why? Why? Why?

This ardor. This unexpected solitude. This sense of absence, of bitter deception. This pain. This desperation. God knows that I would want to fall for ever in the sea of forgetfulness. Any other state would be better compared to this moment of bereavement. Jacques. I am hurt to death.

Jacques. Why? Why? Why?

On the following night Jacques came to visit her. He knew how to make his way to her room and came without announcing himself, undetected by her parents. She was still in confusion, raging resentment. She was not a submissive woman. So she began a sour discussion between them, including fingernails bruising white skin, and lips locked together after so many years. They made love to each other, partially because she didn't have the force to stop him, and partially because she wanted it to happen. She had gone over the reencounter once and again, she had dreamt about this moment for so long, that she just could not stop it.

But when it was over, there was resentment, love and hate, wrapped together. A very uncomfortable situation it was, because she was unable to imagine herself making love to another man.

That was the beginning of a secret romance, until both Mathilde and Jacques' wife became pregnant at the same time. Jacques managed the matter astutely, convincing his cousin and friend Gérard, a quadroon Mulatto, to assume the paternity of the child, marry Mathilde and tolerate the romance. As compensation he would receive a nice hacienda.

Mathilde's family opposed violently to her marriage on the base that it would be a backward leap in the process of lifting the family's color, but when she told her mother that she was pregnant the discussions ceased and the marriage took place with all honors.

For Jacques the situation was more than convenient. No one was surprised to see him spending so much time at Gérard's home, since the town considered them all to be just members of a big extended family, and in any case, rich and well educated people. In addition, all of them had been friends since childhood. So with the tolerance of the husband the romance continued.

Mathilde devoted many days to Jacques' two children. She loved them dearly, and treated them both as her own, and of course the boys liked it that way. In any event, Jacques'wife was an alcoholic. She was never sober. So both children clung on to Mathilde. Her own son thriving on her motherly love, the other finding in her the mother that he didn't have. Her love for Jacques seemed to flourish, as she gradually accepted her fate. Sometimes she trembled while caressing the boys, trying hard not to think about Jacques.

But one night, Gérard had two visitors, Jean Baptise Yayá and Vincent Ogé. They were leading a campaign about equal rights for all citizens of the colony. They were able to kindle such ideals in Gérard, to the point of getting him affiliated to the Movement for Mulattos' Rights. According to Ogé many of the Mulattos were well prepared, with sound economic resources, better education and more civilized that many Whites. But Jean Baptise Yayá was the most convincing. He had eloquence, and a great sense of loyalty toward Ogé. It was evident that he could be the head of the movement. However, he consistently recognized Oge's leadership.

So far, so good! But when Gérard began his new and unexpected activism, she insisted that they should distance themselves from Ogé, especially after he suggested that Gérard should put an end to her secret romance with Jacques. The secret, he said, was by now part of the daily gossips of Saint Dominique.

Gérard counter attacked:

- If Jacques love you as much as he says he does, then he should have married you. He could have followed the example of Paul Boudet that married a Black woman. The color of her skin didn't matter. And if he did not have the guts, at least he could have remained single as so many other French men does, and take you to his home to be his house keeper. But let me put it this way: you are my wife. So this is becoming a disgrace to me.

Mathilde tossed her own resentment on him.

- You should have thought of that long time ago. But your greed for Jacques' lands and my father's wealth made you sell out your dignity.

- Jacques' lands? Those are my uncle's lands. We both are nephews of the same uncle and the two of us have the same rights. See the point? How come I am as good an heir as he is and yet I have to be humiliated in this way? And as far as your father is concerned, he is a decent man whom I appreciate very much, and what I did was to defend his honor, covering up this matter. His own daughter planned his downfall bringing misfortune and disgrace on his house, having no consideration for his gray hair.

She attempted what she had always done since a child, physically assaulting Gérard as she did with Jacques. But he took out his sword and ordered her to be quite.

The situation got very tense in the next few days. And passion could no longer contain resentment. She confronted Jacques again, in an open and direct manner, concerning his betrayal.

A few nights later one of the house slaves came running totally alarmed and screaming.

- Madame, Madame, Madame, your husband and Messier Jacques are about to kill each other.

Mathilde ran after him and arrived to the patio on time to listen to a sour and insulting discussion between the two men about the rights of the Mulattos, France, freedom, equality and fraternity. Both discussed with their hands resting on the handle of their short swords. She knew them too well, so she was not taking any risk. Screaming, she intervened just as the men drew their swords. She looked at Jacques with total desolation and fainted.

The incident was the last straw. Gérard prohibited any relationship between the couple. Contrary to what she expected, the absence of her lover was not that painful. What tore her apart was the memory of that night, the bitter words uttered by both men, but especially the despising attitude coming from Jacques.

So after all it seemed that Jean Baptist Yayá was right when he spoke about the situation of the Mulattos. They had French blood running in their veins, French education, as was the case of Ogé who studied in Paris, financed by his own Black mother; French ideology, as was also the case of Ogé, who had become a personal friend of Brissot, of

Gregoire, of Robespierre, of Lafayette, a militant in the Amis des Noirs group, who were sympathizers of the Black cause in revolutionary France.

- We are their children, uncles, granddaughters, cousins, and supposedly their friends –Jean Baptist said, but yet these White Creoles have made themselves into a separate race blending greed and stupidity. Many blacks have education and properties already, and they will also have access to freedom first and their children to citizenship, because they have the same blood in their veins as the Mulattos.

Jacques, in his fury, could not contain his true self any more. That night he declared bluntly that all Mulattos were bastards, good for nothing, and traitors. So Jean Baptist was right. One could not rely on the White Creoles, because they had no respect for their own relatives.

But Mathilde did miss her adopted son. The son of the French Lady. She and her own son suffered his absence in silence.

Then in October the dreaded Mulatto uprising occurred, led by Ogé. More than two hundred men challenged the colonial power. Ogé was counting on the support of the French revolutionaries. The objective of the movement was clear and very concrete: citizenship for the Mulattos, the same rights as those of the Creole Whites, the same political and economical conditions.

The White colonial population reacted with great forcefulness. Gérard barely managed to escape to the mountains and Ogé and Jean Baptist Yayá fled to the Spanish side of Santo Domingo. But the Spanish authorities returned all prisoners.

Mathilde took refuge in the house of her parents, who went to Port au Prince and put themselves under military protection. Hate and resentment was unleashed against the Mulattos. The idea of "the bastards taking power" was absolutely repulsive and unthinkable on the part of the Creoles.

In March, after being sentenced by the Council, Ogé and Jean Baptist Yayá were led to the square, their feet and hands tied to four energetic horses and quartered. Later, their dying bodieswere exposed in the sun, "for the remaining time in which God wants to conserve their lives" the judge said, giving a clear message to the Mulattos that any one daring from now on to lift the flag of equality would have to face a similar fate.

Te Deum was held in the cathedral, in thanksgiving for the victory of law and order. These are the same laws of God for every one –the Bishop said in his inspiring sermon –and all should obey, following the example of the Holy Virgin Mary and all the other saints.

Jacques never forgave Eduard. First, the house slave had alerted Gérard of his secret intention to go to Mathilde's room and even had the insolence to block his entrance, sword in hand. Two nights after the incident with Gérard, he attempted to speak with Mathilde, to explain to her what had really happened, to let her become aware about how great a traitor his cousin and pal had become and that all that he had said was really directed to him and not to the whole Mulatto race. But Eduard told him that to get to Mathilde's room he would have to make it over his dead body, and the worst part was that other slaves supported him. Something very worrisome was happening: a complete loss of respect for the sacred values of the Saint Dominique society. So, amid the resonant victory of the Creoles, he set out for vengeance, only to find Gérard's home already in flames. He swore that that was the work of Eduard as well and organized a systematic manhunt. He captured Eduard's father, a very old man, his uncle's former coachman, who "so many times lifted up the little master and put him into the carriage" the older people remarked bitterly, and without further thought hanged him in the patio. His lover had also fled, and that hurt him very much.

Later, news came that Mathilde and her family were refugees in Port au Prince and he proposed to capture them. It was not his intention to kill any of them, but his ego demanded that he take them under his custody. He would assign the parent's house for jail and install Mathilde in his own house like a governess of his son; that is, the son of his legitimate wife, and would then raise the other child in his home.

He had to postpone his intention, since he was very busy deliberating in the Council about the possibility of recognizing English sovereignty over the Island. The French flag was trampled and burnt in the square by the indignant Creoles, in repulsion of the ordinances from France giving citizenship to the Mulattos and free Blacks. But in August, when finally things calmed down a little, Jacques got an order from a judge to arrest Mathilde's family for debts. That was just before the Black insurrection.

The news of the rising of the blacks brought panic to all groups. The Mulattos, including Gérard, requested weapons. He himself came out of hiding, and showed up with fifty Mulattos, claiming a place in the ranks of those who were fighting to suppress the Black insurrection.

Jacques, blinded by his recently acquired power, captured Gérard, and in front of the whole troop and the Mulattos that accompanied him, spat on his face, and had him lashed until he admitted that he was one of the instigators of the revolution, along with Ogé and Jean Baptist Yayá and as such, an enemy of France.

But Gérard managed to shout that the traitors of France were the servants of the British, in clear allusion to the conduct of the Creoles in the first weeks after the ordinance that gave citizenship to Mulattos and freed Blacks. This infuriated Jacques, who then ordered his men to cut off his legs and leave him in the patio so that the dogs could lick his blood, and later to cut him up into pieces and feed his flesh to the dogs.

The order was carried out strictly and although during the night some of Gérard's followers were able to flee, others were tortured and shot the following day.

Eduard, under the command of The Bookman was now a prominent member of the Black revolution. The morning after Gérard death, the Black troops advanced on the town, facing bayonets and cannonballs, giving their lives and taking lives.

At first they killed all Whites, including women and children. The Bookman wanted blood, because he said that was the only form of vindicating the race. The insults of two hundred years had to be washed in blood. This was essential, The Bookman said, in order to achieve total purification. Saint Dominique was a den of beasts; and only fire could clean the demons out, the terrible bad spirits that possessed the Whites, he said.

So as they advanced, nothing was left on foot; that which would not burn, was destroyed. Nothing should be left to remember the heartbreaking scene of Eduard's father hanging on the wall, exposed to vultures with a stone hanging from his testicles; a very cruel way to meet death in the hands of the very same boy he had taken care of when his lazy father died; that man who —the old ladies commented —had been such a nuisance to the family, spending his time writing poetry and talking about his rich family from Nantes.

The Bookman and his forces advanced along the road, killing the White children, the very same babies that had been breastfed with love by the Black Mammies, the same children that had been cooed in rhythmic melodies by the domestic slaves, the very same boys and girls that had been fed, bathed and sheltered by devoted Black hands.

They advanced along the road, killing the White women, the same women that had been humiliated by their White husbands, because the gentlemen preferred the Black Woman, making them the ladies in bed; but the White women held on to the rings proudly, bearing White children so that the domain of the White race could continue, keeping them separated from their Black brothers and sisters, so that White preeminence would go on. The same White women, who, once their children were born, trusted them to Black Nannies for their upbringing, so that the children grew and became old enough to repeat the old story of getting married to White women but in private loving or raping Black women.

They advanced alongside the road, until they reached Jacques' home, desiring to avenge Gérard's humiliation, ignoring the fact that he never sided with the Blacks. They killed all those that resisted, including the few slaves that didn't immediately support the revolution. Jacques was not around, so they had it out on his wife. She was raped by a volunteer publicly, and after burning the house, they fled to the mountains.

Jacques led the Creole troops against the Mulattos that had taken refuge in Croix. He went after them with full force, with all the soldiers that he managed to gather, some two hundred men, with heavy armaments and much ammunition. They advanced all night. The following morning they were in the sugar cane plantation, which according to his spies was the refuge of the rebels, but the enemy was not visible.

He ordered his troops to rest, and was about to take breakfast when he saw the first flames. Immediately he raised his voice in alarm, but it was late. Flames surrounded the troops in three directions. There was only one way to escape sure death, and that was to cross the stream over to the other side of the canyons where the Mulattos were supposed to be. They hardly had crossed the stream when the Mulatto troops attacked them, provoking disorder in the Creole lines. They didn't force them to surrender, but rather allowed them to congregate on the other bank of the river, and then forced them to negotiate and sign a treaty that recognized the rights of the Mulattos, expel the judges that had condemned Ogé and Jean Baptist Yayá from the judicial system and create an integrated militia, with the same number of Whites and Mulattos.

Jacques returned to his Hacienda only to face –in addition to his humiliating defeat the pain of the death of his son and the denigration of his wife. Jacques cried like a boy, hating himself for having signed the treaty. In so little time his world had collapsed. His precious colonial society, with its established order, with its mechanisms of ascent, with its limits defined clearly by the color of skin, every one in his rightful place. The zingres, formed by those who had less than eight Whites among their ancestors and the other combinations, including the sacatra, the griffe, the marabou, the mulâtre, the quadroon, the métis, the mamelouk, the Creole White, the continental White, and of course, the Church, and until recently, the Crown, the perfect society, a society in which people respected hierarchy without the heresies of Robespierre.

He swore vengeance.

And when the news arrived from the Metropolis that they had repealed the ordinance that gave rights to the Mulattos, Jacques immediately propose to repeal the treaty.

The Mulatto took refuge in Port au Prince, where they were attacked by the Creole forces. In panic, the whole Mulatto population retreated towards the beach.

Mathilde tried to hold on to her mother, so that she would not fall off the pier. They clung to a rope, trying to resist the pressure of the masses. The first to fall was her father, along with many others who because of old age could not resist and were easily thrown and trampled by the desperate multitude trying to escape cannonballs directed at that sector of the city. The Mulatto militia fought with courage, but was overwhelmed by Jacques' forces.

Mathilde had lost all contact with her son. She did manage to tell him to make his way to the mountains. By now, because of internal disputes among the blacks, The Bookman had been executed, and the new leader Toussaint L' Overture had stopped the killing of women and children. They now also accepted Mulattos in their ranks, and there was a rumor that even Creole White was to be accepted. Mathilde and her family knew the new leader personally. He was one of the famous Black slaves that got their freedom when their masters fled to Louisiana. He had been educated by a famous priest by the name of Pierre Baptiste, whom the free Black population called Father Yayah. He was very well known in the family, because his master was a client. Mathilde wrote a letter to Toussaint and sewed it into the boy's shirt and had him flee toward the mountains with a faithful slave.

But now, the crowd in panic continued pushing, pressing, trampling.

"We could have made a country, Jacques. My father was an Octoroon, and he administered your family's business properly. Thanks to his hard and honest work you were able to study in France. He had served you well, Jacques. In this part of the island, we are all relatives, Jacques. The whole educated population is related, Jacques. All of us have the blood of Whites, the education of the Whites, Black mask, and upbringing of Black women. We could have solved this, Jacques. You see, all that Gérard wanted, all that Jean Baptist Yayá, all that Ogé wanted was a space for us. That was all.

A space for us, Jacques; because I loved you dearly. Because you loved me, without doubt, you loved me. But your big White-male pride did not allow you to marry me. But I know you well. We were raised together. We have loved each other intensely since childhood. But now, hate has blinded you. The thirst of vengeance has put a blindfold over your eyes.

Why?

This ardor. This unexpected solitude. This sense of absence, of bitter deception. This pain. This desperation. God knows that

*I would love to fuse into your existence. I would like to hold you
again, just before I fall for ever into forgetfulness. It is this bitter
existence, this hole. And it hurts. Jacques. Jacques. Mom is about
to fall into the sea and she will surely die. So listen to me for the
last time —you are marking our gravesite. We will all die, but I
will plunge into the sea carrying with me this everlasting love.*

MARIANA

"Your country's freedom is more valuable than your personal life", I told them. "But your life and the life of your children will be invaluable when Cuba becomes a free and independent country. So get down on your knees." I had them go down on their knees: "swear, I told them, swear by the Blood of Jesus ... swear to fight with no rest until your country is free, and independent, or you are dead."

Detail of a portrait by Antonio Guerrero (Toda la patria está en la mujer. Exhibit).

JOSÉ Martí stood on the open corridor. In front of the small tropical home was the road and on the other side of the road the blue and bright waters of the Jamaican sea.

As he stood waiting for doña Mariana Grajales to receive him, he took out his note pad and wrote down an idea that he would later develop for doña Mariana's epitaph: "There is no true Cuban heart that does not feel that we owe our very lives to this woman. If at any moment I feel my strength failing, all I have to do is to remember Mariana...She is..."

The Black Matron came out in the company of Maria Cabrales, Antonio's wife. José stood for a moment in awe, literally engulfed by the welcoming smile on the women's face; Mariana, well into her eighties, brown skin, grey and white hair, sparkling with life.

- Poet —she said, welcome to my home. Welcome to the place I call home at this moment.

- Señora...

- It's Mariana...just Mariana.

- Mariana... Thank you for receiving me.

She smiled even more openly. She was well known as the "Black Smiling Lady, who never cries."

- Maria, she said. José seems very thirsty to me. What about some drinks?

- Of course...In a moment —Maria replied, as she made her way back into the house.

- Did you have a nice trip?

- Yes, all was well. No problem. As usual, keeping out of the reach of the Spaniards.

- Ah, that is our life. That is how we live.

José looked through the window into the living room and he could see a portrait of General Antonio Maceo hanging on the wall.

- And what about Antonio? —He asked —Any news?

- Oh, my boy Antonio! The poor man is frantic. He has been going around from place to place. Haiti, here in Jamaica, Panama, now in Honduras, talking about moving to Nicoya in Costa Rica. But he will not be at rest until he returns to Cuba, whether to conquer or to die.

Maria came back with the drinks, and the three of them sat down together on the fresh, breezy corridor.

- So tell me, José… what's cooking? That is what the Jamaicans say —she was now smiling maliciously.

- A good stew — Marti answered, wholeheartedly matching her enthusiasm. —I have been going around myself; a lot of agitation; trying to raise money; trying to cook a good stew. We must continue the struggle.

Her eyes lighted up. She stood and went over to the veranda. An elderly man went by. As he passed before the Maceos' home, he turned and waved to them.

- Good morning Miss Marian —he said.

She waved back, uttering some words that José could not understand but brought a big smile to the gentleman's face.

- That old man is a true Yayah, a Jamaican Maroon —she said. He reminds me of Guillermo Moncada.

- Ah, name them…Pedro Martínez Freire, Antonio Maceo, Vicente García, José Maceo, Guillermo Moncada… heroism, integrity…beyond race and color.

She turned around and now, facing Marti, sighed.

- The Sprit of Yara… -she said. The Spirit of Yara. It lives on.

- I can only feel shame when I hear some of our leaders complain. I mean, you people. You went on for ten years... Imagine! Ten years of war.

- That's nothing. Think about the Maroons, the CubanMaroons.

José Martí sipped from the glass and fell into introspection. He had studied her life: her parents fleeing from the violence of the Haitian Revolution, looking for a new haven; her husband, fleeing Coro, Venezuela, where his family had fought under the banner of Spain.

- I was born in the revolution. All my life I have been immersed in this struggle. I was born in the turmoil caused by José Antonio Aponte's rebellion...

- The so-called Cuban Spartacus.

- Yes, a valiant man. They executed him without mercy. And then there was the Palenque de Frijol war, where the runaway slaves fought their heads off, while the urban mulattos did nothing, and the White creoles celebrated their execution. And then there was Ventura Sanchez's cry, "Cuba, land of liberty." And in the midst of that entire struggle, I can still remember seeing the enslaved Black bozales being marched through Santiago, naked, chained, humiliated, and scorned by everyone. We had a good position in our family. Not rich, but a good situation...

- And yet you used to visit the detained Maroons –Martí interrupted.

- Our fate is clearly tied to theirs. Those visits helped me not to forget. Antonio was born in the middle of the Matanzas and Havana uprisings, and the cruel reaction of the Spanish colonial government was against us all. Whether we were free, Maroons or slaves, it didn't matter to them. Marcos had to buy a birth certificate, presenting himself as born in Santiago.

- Well, Mariana, the fight is not over. I need your help. I need Antonio's help.

- Write to him, he is in Honduras; a commander in the Honduran army.
- I wrote to him. I told him I would be stopping in Port Limon, Costa Rica, but I got no answer.
- Well, guess he may have to think about it. You see... your friends, the moderates...This goes all the way back to the Reformist Party. They use to be strong advocates of autonomy and even independence but had nothing to say about freedom from slavery.
- But Antonio knows that I am a radical and outspoken opponent of slavery.
- Well, let me tell you the story...Wait one second.
She went into the house and brought out a small badge with a Mason sign on it.
- This belonged to Marcos...
- Your husband.
- Yes. Same problem in Coro: the Maceos were Venezuelan Pardos and yet, loyal to the Spanish crown, considering the local White and Mestizo Creoles more threatening. At least the Spaniards were promising liberty to the slaves. And Cuba...Aye, Cuba! Marcos organized the forces of Majaguabo. Then came the Cry of Yara.
- Yes, they said you made them swear...
- Well, I had my own army at home...You know I had ten children of my own and six from my second husband.
- They said you made them go down on their knees.
Mariana broke out into laughter.
- Yes, I made them swear: all of my children. I made them swear.
- But they say it was not only the family...
The venerable Matron was now in a laughing fit. José went on with her. At that moment he had another glance at one of the most famous traits of her personality, immortalized in the popular saying: "Mariana, the smiling Black Lady, who never cries."

- So you got them all to swear...

- Yes. When Manuel de Céspedes and Juan Rondon got their revolutionary forces together...I don't know, I had never seen so many men together in all my life. It must have been some five hundred and fifty men, including the guajiros...I got them down on their knees right there at Las Delicias and had them swear. "Your country's freedom is more valuable than your personal life", I told them. "But your life and the life of your children will be invaluable when Cuba becomes a free and independent country. So get down on your knees." I had them go down on their knees: "swear, I told them, swear by the Blood of Jesus who was the first liberal in the history of this earth, and swear to fight with no rest until your country is free and independent, or you are dead."

She burst out into laughter again.

- Your Mambi revolutionaries were the best —José said, and added —and your son Antonio...

- Oh yes, all of them. My husband, and here, my beloved daughter in law, in reality, Maria is just another daughter. I mean, the women! They all had to be strong...

- Tell him about the skirt issue —Maria said jokingly, but Mariana only continued laughing briskly.

- Tell me...tell me —José invited.

- It was one of those hard days when we were attending to the wounded. Some of our women broke out crying... Mariana got into a fit, and shouted to us: "there is no place for skirts here. No time for crying. Listen to me: either you help the men get well, so that they can get back into battle, or get the hell out of here."

Mariana was now laughing and clapping her hands.

- And tell him about Marcos —Maria continued.

- What about Marcos?

- Your son Marcos. You know what she did? Miguel -one of her sons- was wounded, badly wounded, and this woman here shouted to her other son, the poor frightened fourteen year old Marcos: "it is time for you to go to the camp and take his place."

- Oh, well. I went around with the Mambi troops. I didn't stay home. The Spaniards would have hanged me any way. You know they would. But Antonio...Antonio...Antonio... He is the bravest of us all.

- I know, I know...that's why we need him. He is a natural leader...and a military genius.

- Glad to hear you say so. Not every one thinks that way... Some still believe that Antonio is leading a "Black Revolution" of some sort. There are those who have refused to serve under his command. Maceo has never wanted to set up a Black Republic. He wants to see Cuba free and all Cubans equal. That includes Black and White Cubans. Look at his ranks: all colors, he never makes any kind of distinction, ever...And yet look what Flor Crombet did. He was rude and abusive. He went so far as to push Antonio to the point where he had no choice but to challenge him to a duel. We are lucky that some reasonable people persuaded them to leave the duel for another time. Cubans must put aside social distinctions, dissension, and fight for freedom. Freedom from Spanish rule. Freedom from slavery. Freedom from racial prejudice. We have to get rid of this seed of discord: it is our disgrace.

- I agree with you. And I believe we are succeeding. For me Antonio is indispensable to Cuba. I mean this sincerely. I feel a deep and intimate affection for your son. He has been the greatest.

Doña Mariana came close to José and took his hand. She held his hands in hers, squeezing them, rubbing them tenderly.

- Maria —she said —Please tell our people to come over. They must hear José's message. Tell them my son José

Martí will be speaking tonight. Use those words: "Mariana's son, José Martí." And ask Miss Williams for help. In the meanwhile I'll set the table. Your brother José will dine with us. And we will have a toast for Cuba's freedom.

The Panther

(QDM. Liberty Hall, UNIA, Limón)

I said. "Amy, is kill, them kill him, you noh!"

- No –Amy said... No one can kill Marcus. When a person dies he is not really dead. His Spirit will live on in us.

FRANKLY speaking he didn't expect the medical service to be mobilized with so much ease. But this is London, power's cradle. Racism, of course; although it can be alleged that it did not begin here. In fact, it began on the Continent, in the Alcalá University, to be more specific, where the cultured monks devised the fundamental theology as they debated whether the Native American people had souls. And they continued building racism in the name of God until the Pope finally stated that all human beings had been created by God, all had the same origin, and all had souls. It was a bit too late. In Germany, the United States and Britain, they had begun the "scientific" construct later known as social Darwinism, and had paved the road to hell. So the Portuguese took over the task of imposing captivity with fury on the Africans, as if that was their sole destination in life. This they did in spite of the thousand Black welders that came to them from the Moors, and the million farmers that taught the non tropical Europeans how to cultivate tropical food.

These had been the things debated with Marcus so many times. French and Germans, Norwegian and Dutch, Belgians and of course the Englishmen, went into Africa, to seize everything they could, including the food and the people, trying hard to also take the people's dignity. Bantu dignity. Ashanti dignity. Zulu dignity. Yoruba dignity. Yayah dignity.

Trying hard to rob our humanity, to leave us without the soul that God Almighty put in our bodies.

But yes, they are on the rush. Totally unexpected. I guess these Englishmen are wise enough to perceive that if Marcus dies in London, his death will be an embarrassment to the Royal Government. How will they explain it to the Black community in such a way that it makes sense to them and to History?

It was at that very moment when it occurred to me that they had poisoned Marcus. There was no other possible explanation. He was fine earlier when he walked into this elegant building. He was just all right. I have been close to him over the years and I can live up to that statement. I was with him debating the convenience or not of becoming a Member of Parliament, a wild proposal which I would say was never feasible, but one simple intended to distract Marcus' indomitable drive for freedom.

So here they are, fighting for his life and I don't believe them. To save him from the death that they themselves are causing would be absolutely absurd. This was the destruction that they had attempted so many times. Since he was a boy, they had done everything possible to break his will, and they have not been able to. So why should they stop now?

When we were growing up together, walking the little town roads, neither Marcus nor I knew about these things. We were free and happy then, playing with the daughter of the Missionary and with my cousin. Marcus was the blackest of the group, the daughter of the Missionary was totally white; my cousin's skin was like cinnamon and he had green eyes with remarkable Ashanti features. My hair was like that of the Asian Indians. But nothing of that mattered when we were growing up together in Jamaica. We were inseparable friends and to tell the truth, Marcus was a bit in love with the Missionary's daughter, who corresponded enthusiastically.

So they decided to put an end to paradise. They gave you the first blow. And it was these same colonial Englishmen that are now trying to convince us that they want to save your life. The Missionary said that it was time to return to England, to make sure that his daughter would continue in the path of a respectable English Family. But he did say a lot more in private, and literally ignored Hindi Jane, who listened to the conversation. He told his wife that if they were to expect his daughter to become the wife of a gentleman, she should not be exposed any longer to the rather worthless colonial life. And of course, the growing friendship with this Garvey boy was a matter of concern. The Missionary's wife listened to him attentively, over a very pleasant breakfast, immediately after the blessing of the food. She shared the concern but felt that the matter could be solved by speaking to the young lady. In a way, according to Hindi Jane, the point was that in Jamaica she was a Lady, while back home she would be just another one of those women whose only letter of presentation was that she had been to the colony. But the Pastor insisted that that would be only a temporary solution; that the solution to the dilemma could only come through a complete reinsertion of the girl into English society. In any case, he had already completed the Work of the Lord, according to his own criteria, and it was time to return to the Motherland, get himself a comfortable position in a good parish and enjoy the benefits of his effort.

So they snatched our English friend away, imposing on us two categories which we did not choose ourselves –them and us. Us and them. And it has remained that way since then. So there is no possibility, sir, your courtesy not withstanding, of making me your witness. On the contrary, I hereby testify to history, that this was not a natural death. So don't count on me, your Majesty, just don't count on me.

So you see, it was not the only blow. What about Marcus' uncle? That man was our model. He was the manager of a large farm. In fact, he didn't have his own farm like Marcus' father did.

So he leased a former slave farm and made and lost his fortune obstinately battling the system. He had converted the abandoned property of the grandson of one of the former masters of the island into a valuable farm. The young White lad who owned the property, frankly speaking, was a disgrace to the town; poor enough and drunk enough to be exhibited as an example of a very useless and parasitical class that flourished in elegant uselessness, cultivated and inherited over generations.

Being a Garvey as he was, Marcus' uncle boasted the same drive for success. He created an exemplary hacienda on the White man's property, but was finally kicked off by the devoted church-going drunkard that prayed to the Lord every day and read his Bible, drank brandy copiously and did no work.

At a very early age, Marcus left Jamaica following his uncle, who had moved to Costa Rica and established himself in a place called, let me see…Limón. A banana port somewhere in Central America, on the Caribbean coast. There his uncle, being an adventure-some and educated man, held a good position in the Northern Railroad Company, and therefore managed to place his nephew in the offices as a time-keeper.

Marcus thus had the opportunity to experience firsthand the fate of the Jamaicans that had immigrated to the Central American coast. And he did not like what he saw.

That was the case of Joe Gordon. Marcus told me his story. He had heard about Limón, and decided to go there and make a fortune. This was possible for hard-working men, they were told by the company's agents as they recruited workers for Costa Rica. His dream was to work for a few years and return to Jamaica, buy himself a small property, build a house, find a good wife and in keeping with the new times, raise children to be free and independent.

Everything went well at the beginning. But one day, while working on the railroad, Joe, in an effort to save a fellow worker, lost control of one of the boxcars that then derailed. It was a simple thing, instinctive, and it happened in the blink of the eye. Joe was putting on the brake, when a platform collapsed. I believe that was what it was. I don't know much about railroads, so I am using his words. As a consequence, one of the workers was hanging on for his life over the bank of a cliff and Joe, believing that human life was important, ran to save him. Of course his action was considered heroic by the fellow workers but the boxcar derailed and it took a lot of energy and time to repair the damage. The company lost money in that operation, enough to fire Joe. It was that simple. They discharged him because he was more interested in human life than in his obligation as an employee to defend the integrity of the Company's property. Far more important was the profit for the owners back in Boston and the benefit for the consumer eating his banana glasse in a French restaurant in London.

After I heard Joe's story, I decided that Costa Rica was no place for a young Jamaican. I wanted to make my own fortune, but there was not many opportunity in Jamaica either. So I was glad to go along with Marcus to Europe, after he got home from his Central American adventure. I did not tell him this, but I hoped that once in the "Mother Land" I could find the answer to my modest dreams. Because Marcus had been in Panama, in Colombia, Ecuador, Nicaragua and Honduras and everywhere he had encountered the same old story of poor Black people and Indians suffering from oppression. For them independence and freedom had no real meaning.

But while in Costa Rica, Marcus started to return the blows. His local family was not very happy with this. But he had been hit all his life. Now he was returning the blows. He worked hard, publishing his ideas in newspapers such as The Nation in Limón and The Press in Bocas del Toro, Panama, in order to mobilize the Black population to defend their rights. He was concerned about the fact that wherever he went, he could see Black people creating wealth for the White and Mestizo population. So he planned a trip to Europe, searching for the country of the Black popuation, with companies controlled by Blacks, with a government run by Blacks, with schools that would teach the history of the Blacks.

On the way, a copy of Booker T. Washington's book Up from Slavery came to his attention. That book was little and was nothing and was everything. Because it was a small book, written by a man who had been a slave and had lifted himself to the point of founding a remarkable educational institution for Blacks. It was a history of which they could be proud. But the book transformed the life of Marcus and convinced him that his life had just one purpose –he had been born to carry out a single task, to lift the flag of the Black cause.

London was London. We saw more real history and real arrogance than we could dream of. Big Ben. Westminster Cathedral. And it was there, in front of the Empire's monuments that Marcus swore. It was impressive to see him making his way through the city from library to library, from parish to parish, from street to street, from monument to monument. I was worried because I interpreted his enthusiasm as a fascination for the greatness of his Majesty's Empire. It seemed to me that he was being converted into a devoted Englishman, and that we were losing ground.

But then, he swore.

I swear that I heard him swearing, right there in the very heart of the Old Empire, in the shrine where humanity at that moment was forging history. He swore, in front of all those symbols of imperial greatness that he would devote his life to the creation of that Black Country he dreamt about. And his face was transformed, and his eyes were shining like they never had since he was a boy.

- I swear- he said with absolute solemnity- that I will not rest until we have created the country of the Blacks, until we have recovered the soul of the Blacks, until we have rewritten the history of the Blacks.

On our way back to Jamaica –we traveled in second class – we met a Jamaican that had married an African Woman from the Yayah Country. He told the same story of oppression. And I saw my dreams collapsing. But Marcus on the other hand seemed to grow with each new story, possessed by his conviction that change is possible.

He founded the United Negro Improvement Association, and we traveled intensively through Jamaica in search of support. We spoke first with the influential Mulatto class only to see doors being slammed on us. We then went to the churches, to the pastors, to the teachers.

- Yes, the cause is just –they all said –but it is not wise that the movement be headed by a Black radical. A trouble maker. If he was a brown-skinned man, you see what I mean? A fair gentleman.

Later, the Governor put Garvey in jail, accusing him of being an agitator. The Mulattos celebrated this.

- We told you, he is nothing but a trouble maker, a worthless agitator and an uncultured person.

This was the most stupid thing that they could have said about him because I doubt that there was any one of his age on the whole Island of Jamaica that had read as much as he had. And it was not only the culture and the many countries that he had visited; it was his awareness that counted most.

Garvey wrote to Booker T. Washington. He was fed up with the resistance of the educated elite in Jamaica, in whom the Empire had achieved the most complete of all conquests, which is the conquest of the mind. They thought like Englishmen, reciting the poem of the Charge of the Six Hundred with pride, affirming the brilliant feat ofAdmiral Nelson at Trafalgar, recognizing the civilizing force of Great Britain. They had been woven into the culture, and had become themselves blind to the suffering, insensible to the dead, ignoring torture, taking refuge in the Churches, choosing not to remember the suffering of flesh and blood, the cruel bitterness and the barbarism of a civilization that if for some was life for others was agony and death.

Fed up with them, Marcus and I undertook the trip to the United States, in order to converse with Booker and to undertake the universal movement together. But fate took Booker's life before our arrival and therefore the encounter that could have marked the destiny of humanity never occurred.

But the years of glory began. The years in which Marcus lifted an emporium of four hundred thousand blacks all over the world, and bought ships and founded the Black Star Line, and our own branch of the Orthodox Church, and the Black Nurses and Black schools and issued the Declaration of the Rights of the Black People and established Black Day, and marched in the company of thousands down the streets of New York, and twenty thousand congregated to hear the word of the Black Panther there in Limón, the very same Limón in which he had lived and worked. Beyond the betrayal forged by the Government of Liberia in alliance with the Goodyear Company, when trying to establish his headquarters in that country, beyond everything, Marcus, vital, powerful, Prophet, Leader…You don't beg for your rights, you take them. And we are entitled to build ours by any means that we esteem viable.

Now they are killing you; that White doctor, with his white hair, his white magic, his white smile. Because it is not appendicitis, Amy, it is not peritonitis. Heroes die standing; I said. "Amy, is kill, them kill him, you noh!"

- No —Amy said, speaking in the tone of an authentic Yayah woman —Marcus has returned us to life. New Life. No one can kill Marcus. When a person dies he is not really dead. His Spirit will live on in us.

YOUNG MARTIN

- Mom, why?

- Why what?

- Why do we have to live on that side of the city and they live over here?

YOUNG Martin lifted his face in order to contemplate the enormous buildings. The truth is that they were frightening. Amid that mass of cement and glass, characteristic of that side of the city, he felt smaller than ever. From time to time his mother looked at him. He always thought that she was a very big woman, and he admired her for that reason. But amid the buildings, she was looking small. Very small.

- Mother –he said, why are all the people white in this part of the city?

His mother smiled.

- And in our part of the city everyone is black.
- Yes, that's true. Why?
- Because we live there and they live here.
- How come?
- Well, would you like to live here among White people? I know you would.
- No, no. Why do you say that?
- So, well?

In fact that was not the point. But they were arriving at the corner and it was necessary to cross the wide street and that got him nervous because the automobiles were always in a hurry. They got over the other side of the street, and she was about to say something to make sure she didn't have to continue coping with the issue. But young Martin would not let it go.

- Mom, why?

- Why what?

- Why do we have to live on that side of the city and they live over here?

She began to get nervous. It was not the right place, being in the cave of the lion, to have such a discussion.

- Martin, can we talk about this later? Right now you see, I have to think about finding our way back home.

- Well, alright Mama.

Mrs. King sighed deeply. She breathed the rancid air of the city and she thought about her parents and grandparents and about her great grandparents. What was an appropriate answer for her son? Maybe this was the most important question he would ever ask, or maybe it was nothing. The Lord knows what would have been the easiest answer, but she new her son would not accept it. Nature came to her rescue —Martin wanted to urinate.

- You have to wait until we get over the line. We are close. On the other side we can sit down and have a soda and you can go to the rest room.

- I don't want soda, I want to pee.

- Wait, boy. Give me a break. We're close to the line.

- Mama, why do I have to pee at the line? Why can't I just pee here?

- What do you mean, here? Here on the street?

- No I mean…look, there is a hotel over there. They'll let me use the bathroom.

She was becoming angry over a situation she could not handle.

- No, they won't. So you are going to have to wait. You can't pee this side of the city.

Martin was totally confused. On this side there are no restrooms, he thought for a moment, maybe White people on this side of the city don't pee. Any how, he could not stand the urge any longer, so he broke away from his mother and ran towards the hotel. He didn't give her time to react. He ran directly through the door and on up to the counter.

- Ma'am- he asked the receptionist –would you please lend me your restroom so that I can pee? –he asked politely.

- Get him out of this place! –the woman shouted to the bellboy who was already making his way to the counter. He was Black, and there was anguish all over his face.

- Come on boy, you have to leave.

- All I want is to pee.

- Well you can't pee here. Come.

He took Martin by the arm and escorted him out of the hotel, where his mother stood in desperation.

- Is this your child?

- Yes sir.

- Well Lady, take him and educate him. You know your place. Teach him.

- Yes sir.

Mrs. King nagged at her son severely.

- You see: you almost got us into trouble.

- You should come on into the place. The lady would lend you the restroom so that I could pee.

The boy was furious, resentful, claiming out loud that he did not like to sit at the back of the bus and he did not want to go to the line to pee.

After a while, he calmed down.

- Mom, he said, you are a good person. You are a good person.

- Well, thank you…

- My father says that you can convince anybody. Why didn't you help me out?

- I could not enter there son, it is prohibited

- Why?

- Because I am Black. Black people cannot go into those places.

- But mom, the bellboy is Black.

She heard voices in her head. Like God was speaking to her. But they were not English words. It had to do with a person whose name was Nsinga, and it had to do with the Yayah people, and there was something about a town called Acompong, and another thing about the region of Santo Tomé. And oh, that is it. It is about Brother Garvey,

"Please Lord, she whispered, help me with this one."

To use the name of the Lord was a big mistake, because now young Martin had another question. It was about "never seeing White people in our Church."

She felt like dying.

- But Jesus is White.

- No he was not White. He was Jewish.

By now she was sobbing. There was not a place in history for her son, no place in theology. And she went totally pale when her son could not help himself any more and wet his pants.

The boy was crying now. "Mama —he said, some one has to change this. Some one has to."

"Precious Lord", Mrs. King murmured to herself with all the force she could muster, "have mercy upon us."

THE GERMAN DOCTOR

The order came directly from higher ranks, so there was no possible way to appeal: "all Blacks in Germany must be sterilized". For that reason, that dreadful morning when Peter came to get her, Abby followed in apathy, all the way to Peter's clinic. This was her brother in Christ, her pew-partner, the same very young boy with whom she shared her first kiss. She just went along, avoiding eye contact, not a word said, and closed her eyes just before chloroform.

I heard the story from my grandmother. Both men were sitting in the canteen, with a jar of beer before them and a mug for each.

- But Francois, it is not worth it...

- I just can't take it.

- But I mean, you are in a good position now. A good marriage. A good job. You are all ok. Why throw every thing away? I mean, it's stupid.

- You don't understand. As long as I didn't know the guy he was never really real to me. But now I know him, that damn conceited bastard! I hate his guts. You have no idea how it is not being able to have a child.

- Come on, Francois, you can have a child.

- She can't.

- Well, but, I mean...

- I want her to be my child's mother.

- Oh come on, for God's sake, you were well aware of the situation before you married Abby. She told you. How come you suddenly want to have it out on him over something that took place such a long time ago? Instead of helping her get over it, you are sprinkling salt into the wounds.

- You just don't get it. I knew she couldn't have a child. Of course I knew that. But I had not met Peter. Now I know the guy, the monster finally has blood and flesh. I hate his guts.

Francois was not a direct witness of his mother-in-law's tears that morning, when Peter came to get Abby along with his thugs. Francois was then in the French army, fighting against the ominous regime that classified them as subhuman. First, they revoked grandfather's German citizenship, because it was against the law for any Yayah to be considered German. Then came the exclusion of Abby: she was not to march behind the German flag any more. Soon after the old man died, frustrated, not withstanding his reputation as a kind and compassionate person, and a good Lutheran.

The old man came to Europe to study in his early twenties, but the colonial regime changed and his family was accused of conspiracy. He finally found love, adopted citizenship and made Germany home. So once they took his citizenship away, he just sat on his bed and died, for you cannot live if you loose that much after a life of loyalty. And Abby, after loosing her father, who she loved dearly, was later excluded from her best friend's wedding on racial grounds. A friend lost –including the dreams dreamt together, and the illusions they had shared.

Francois was not there when the town's Jewish family disappeared. The father just banished. The other members, hidden by the community for a while, fled to Poland. Another lost: her father's very best client and good friend, respected even by the Lutheran pastor.

None of us was a direct witness of what happened, but knowing Abby, one can perceive the solemn Yayah dignity with which she faced her adversity. Yes, that ancestral dignity that she herself cannot explain.

The order came directly from higher ranks, so there was no possible way to appeal: "all Blacks in Germany must be sterilized". For that reason, that dreadful morning when Peter came to get her, Abby followed in apathy, all the way to Peter's clinic. This was her brother in Christ, her pew-partner, the same very young boy with whom she shared her first kiss. She just went along, avoiding eye contact, not a word said, and closed her eyes just before chloroform.

But Francois had witnessed Abby's pain. And he would have kept his wits if it had not been for the incident the night before. While attempting to drown his frustration in beer, he met Peter. He had just got a letter explaining why, for the third time, his petition to adopt an African child had been rejected by the government. It was then that someone signaled out to Peter, one of the town's medical doctors. Rather unexpectedly, Peter came to his table, sat down and for no reason started explaining that during the Nazi regime they had "sterilized" Black women. To Francois it was a display of unbearable arrogance.

Froylan, his friend and comrade was trying hard to mitigate his rage.

- It was not an intentional offense. In fact, he just came over and was talking. You didn't let him speak. And the truth is that all that his friends did was to protect him from you. You wanted to kill him right there and then.

- So whose side are you on?

- I am on your side. You know I love you both. I mean, Abby has been my best friend. And I have come to call you brother. So, back off!

- But I mean, you saw what happen. He was trying to impress me with his adventures, the damn red mackerel. I mean, he didn't even show a bit of remorse. I mean, he...he...

He had to stop. He had not been there, then, but he was here now. His wife's pain was now his. His mother-in-law's pain, as she saw her husband die. Her pain, as she saw her dream to watch little brown-skin German children, calling her "Granny", slipping away. Those were all his pain now.

- Please...Froylan begged for the last time.

- Just leave me alone. I'll wait for the beast to come out of it's cave.

Froylan went running desperately across the streets of their small town. Francois's home was not far away and he was convinced that Abby could get her husband to take hold of himself.

As he approached the house, Abby came rushing out in glee and hung on to his neck.

- Froylan —she said —I am pregnant.
- What?
- I am pregnant.
- But...how? You mean...Oh, Jesus, Jesus —he began dragging her and she ran behind him —we have to hurry. Run, I'll explain, but run, run...

They made it just in time to see Peter emerging from his office and Francois coming out of the canteen. Abby ran toward Peter to use her body as a shield. Francois would have placed his shot on the mark as a good soldier would yet he hesitated when he saw his wife standing before Peter. But Peter pushed her away and step towards Francois.

- You son of a...How many Black women did you fixed up?
- Francois, I am pregnant! I am pregnant! -Abby was shouting. But Francois could not stop his rage. He was deft; he was blind except for the image of a medical doctor he hated. He just was not there. He aimed and pulled the trigger at the very moment when Froylan managed to trip him over.

The doctor fell; his wounded feet could not hold his body in its upright position.

No charges were pressed. I know that. My name is Pete. Francois and Abby's only son.

ROSA

-Stay in your place and keep yourself out of trouble. Just get behind the line.

- I would have done exactly that, sir, but I am very tired today.

(Design: "The Bus" by Sebastián Mello and Rafael Sáenz. Featuring Shara Duncan)

ROSA crossed the street almost dragging her feet. Stopping at the bus terminal, she looked toward the end of the street. In any moment a bus would bend that same corner and stop here, exactly where we are. Her heart was beating briskly. It was a strong, unusual beat.

She had been thinking about the passive resistance lecture. It was an interesting strategy, she thought. It had worked for Mahatma Gandhi, but one had to be prepared for sacrifice and bravery. The same pluck it took the Black soldiers of the battle of Milliken's Bend to run toward the canyons and use even their bodies to stop the shootings. Passive resistance, a great thing, so widely preached, so seldom practiced,

The bus came around the corner and, advancing at half speed, stopped abruptly a few steps ahead. The line advanced in an orderly way as usual. But Rosa saw a nice seat. She rushed toward it as if it were a pool of fresh water. It was like going to grandmother's house, and sitting at the table and watching her serve a bowl of gumbo. It was like sitting down in grandfather's lap, listening to the old trickster stories. It was the same sensation of delight that came with jazz flowing from Satchmo's sax. It was like being in Church on a bright Sunday, and while listening to the choir chanting, feel the Plenitude of the Spirit, and slowly, to become another voice in the choir, intoning a deep song, a song of the soul, a song of a thousand years. It was a nice seat and she was very tired. So she sat down.

The bus continued as usual. Nobody noticed, except Sam, that old liar who went around telling people that he was born before the Civil War and had fought next to Lincoln in the Battle of Gumbo Valley. Sam was almost always drunk. Every day he followed the same routine: he would go downtown, hang out at whatever corner he could, dodging from the police to beg for a living. Then, at this hour as usual, he would make it back to the Black zone to spend his money on a good soup at Mrs. Heather's restaurant, and cheap whiskey from the corner bar.

He was well acquainted with Rosa and for that reason recovered total sobriety. He could not believe that she would be sitting in the White area of the bus. He blinked his eyes several time, just to be sure it was not another one of his typical hallucinations. This was definitely real. What was wrong with her? Wasn't she the same lady that he remember taking quilting lessons at —what was that lady from Trinidad's name? Oh, was it Miss Amy Yahman? She was heading for a night in jail or begging to be lynched by the K. K. K. So when the bus stopped and a White man came on the bus, Sam's heart went wild.

As expected, the White man went directly to her and told her in a firm voice to get up. But Rosa did not move. Sam knew that the order was as of Divine Will, that it came directly from the Bible through the mouth of the pastors and the priests, because no Black pastor could ever preach at a White Church and there were neither Black nuns nor bishops. Even the most progressive churches only accepted Blacks seated on the back pews.

- Get up, I want to sit down. But Rosa did not move.

- Nigger, he said —are you deaf? Get up; I want to sit there.

- No, she said —I am tired.

So she's tired. Sam murmured to himself. That is a damn good reason!

The White man was outraged.

- Now, let me put this very clear: get your ass out of my way. But Rosa did not move.

- I am tired. Sit over there.

Rosa looked through the window and suddenly it occurred to her that this was passive resistance. She became aware that without doubt they would arrest her. God knows she had always been a peaceful woman. No big ideas, beyond being a very good worker, a good Christian, a good taxpayer, and not much more than that.

This personal act of rebellion was only that —a very personal act of protest. She was just expressing what she felt. Rosa herself, like dozens of thousands of Blacks before her, had gotten up from the seat and taken their place in the back of the bus. So it was easy; no big deal. All she had to do was to get up and put an end to this senseless bravado. But she did not move. She was very tired.

The man called to the bus driver who, at the next stop came with a true hoodlum attitude.

- Didn't you hear what this man told you? In fact, you should have known. Stay in your place and keep yourself out of trouble. Just get behind the line.

- I would have done exactly that, sir, but I am very tired today.

- Well let me put it this way: I'm not going to argue with you. I am going to have you arrested.

The bus driver returned to his seat and continued his way a couple of blocks and then stopped the bus and got off. A couple of minutes later he returned with two police officers. At the back of the bus, Sam wanted to shout to her, "Lady, for God's sake, move over to the back." He wanted to say, "Miss Rosa, please, it is not worthwhile. It is not worthwhile.

Sam knew that Black men and women fought against slavery and took part in the Civil War, and were brave soldiers in the World Wars. He knew that in all these wars they conducted themselves with discipline, with heroism, and still they return home to humiliation, to being boys as usual. So he doubted that a woman's individual act of rebellion could change the world. So Sam did what he had not done since he was a child: he prayed to God and he proposed a deal:

- Please Lord, save Miss Rosa, please, please save her, and I promise not to drink again. I promise to go to church. I swear God, I swear.

The officials repeated the order, but she did not move, so they arrested her for contempt.

Old Sam wanted to get off the bus, but he could not move from his seat. He sank into apathy thinking that God had failed him. In retaliation, he took out a small bottle of whiskey, which he carried around for emergencies, and sipped generously. But when he arrived at his area of the City, something in his interior drove him to the Pastor's home. It was as simple as that. He informed the Minister about Miss Rosa's heroic act.

That night, he had no time for whiskey. Old Sam was among the Blacks that took to the streets and began stirring up the city. Days later, in his clean suit donated by the Pastor's wife, he had the opportunity to listen to one of Reverend Martin Luther King's sermons. They were to boycott the buses. Right through the sermon he thought about Rosa. It was like Mary and Jesus. She had given birth to a new him.

UNITED COLORS OF BENITO

He slowly approached the "doors" of the city, painstakingly conserved over the centuries. It was a lovely, sunny day, clear sky and blue warm waters. He looked at the two imposing cylindrical structures, located on both sides, as his yacht passed amid them at the exact same moment.

THERE he stood, proudly, on the deck, with all his pride behind him, looking at the imposing entrance to the city. He was about to carry out the dream cherished from boyhood. A dream he built up bit by bit listening to the stories told by his mammy, the woman who reared him. She never stopped speaking about his roots.

And in that regard there was not much to learn from his parents. His mother was a faithful Ebony Magazine reader and that was as "cultural" as her agenda got. Every time the new edition came from the United States with her name labeled on the package, she would lay down forever in the patio hammock with a good selection of cocktails and demanded that nobody interrupted her.

One day he finally confronted his father about his thirst for knowledge only to receive a very simple and direct answer, "the past is gone and you don't need to know about it, because he who dwells in the past is condemned to be stuck in it. And to be stuck in the past, to go on remembering is a damned habit of the Muslims, Jews and worthless Black people, and certainly not a worthwhile occupation."

So it had nothing to do with us. We are the rightful descendants of La Rochelle merchants and for that reason we should look toour French heritage. His father established the distance between himself and his mammy forever.

In the neighborhood, at primary school and later at high school, he had had no problems. In fact, everybody else was like him. Many of the girls from his circle were models of straight nose, cinnamon skin, with an uncontrollable admiration for everything French. Truly enough, there were some couples in which the men were of darker complexion but the women were light skinned, with two exceptions he could recall. And all of them, including the darkest, took a lot of pride in the great Mother Country, even when they had to conform to the honorary condition of overseas citizens.

It was a curious thing that amid that circle of frivolity, with all the money at their disposal, those women were not in charge of their children. The children were reared at the feet and in the laps of the domestic Black employees, which inculcated in their minds, along with respect and affection for the French, many ideas about ancestral roots.

His mammy made no discrimination against his French part. So it was through her that he discovered that on his father's side there was a grandfather from La Rochelle.

- Your grandfather was a member of one of the most distinguished families of France —she would tell him all the time – a trader.

Later he discovered that the people of La Rochelle made their riches by means of the Triangle Commerce, but in vain he tried to get his father to speak.

- Son, forget about the tales of the past. I have told you already that you should get rid of this damn foolish Black oral tradition. That is what keeps them down.

His father said "them" not "us." But he needed to know. It was not a matter of believing that he had the right to suddenly present himself to La Rochelle authorities with a letter of inheritance and a "ces't moi" smile. But maybe he could just walk through the city, take a look at the Museum or the files and search for data that could confirm that one of his ancestors had a place in history; that one of them had been rich, and all of that was genetic and had been handed down from one generation to the other. Because... well, he was prepared to concede that it was a very remote possibility but it was a possibility. His mammy could have been right and all of his father's small fortune was in fact the product of a family inheritance that they should forget, a fortune built on the base of slave trade.

The other side was also there. Those nights when, with the support of his faithful mammy, he escaped from home, to participate in the carnival or in the ceremonies that the Blacks held on certain occasions. He could then feel the blood boiling in his body. Those were his moments of grandeur and freedom. There it was – transfiguration, the recovery of the so called bohemian spirit "de la negritude Yayah." In fact he didn't understand what went on in his mind and definitely could not have defined "Negritude Yayah."

What was clear to him is that at those moments he was liberated from all the tensions and pressure of being an overseas Frenchman. But now, he is the owner of his own life; his yacht approaching the city. He put on a white shirt, his elegant Bermuda shorts; he tied an elegant sweater loosely over his shoulders. He went through his wallet to make sure he had all the necessary documents, including the U.S. American cards, Dinner's Club, Visa, Master Card, American Express, the gold ones, the ones that gave him the distinction that a refined and wealthy person should have at all times. The final line was the unmistakable odor of the very best cologne on the market. He would then stepped out on the deck to face the city.

He slowly approached the "doors" of the city, painstakingly conserved over the centuries. It was a lovely, sunny day, clear sky and blue warm waters. He looked at the two imposing cylindrical structures, located on both sides, as his yacht passed amid them at the exact same moment. He felt a sudden and intense sickness that almost knocked him down on the deck, and forced him to ask for a couple of pills. But the strange feeling continued to grow as his feet stepped onto the pier.

Behind him, the water; above, the sky, the sunbeams and below the stones that have been there from time immemorial. He advanced, with the growing conviction that he knew the city street by street; with his telescopic lens camera hanging from his neck. He entered a narrow passage, with the total awareness that if he opened the gate that was halfway down the way —and he did — there would be a garden —and there was —a breath-taking sight, with every single thing familiar, as if he had been there before, as if he had been a part of it at some remote time, as if they had kept it as it was so that he could remember.

He followed the narrow trail that led through the garden and went towards the other gate, only to find himself on the narrow street again, in this cute little outfit, and the children hollering "cest le Haitian, cest le Haitian" as he plunged down the street, trying to get away from them,

The voice of the leader hauntingly urging the children to prevent his escape, and they caught him and tore off his clothes, but he managed to flee again, in the cold winter morning. Suddenly, as he ran around a curve exactly at the corner, a White boy signaled him to get into a small cave-like hole that led to the interior of a large patio. He was trembling, his lips blue, his nostrils frozen; his eyes wide open in terror. Out on the street he could hear his persecutors' footsteps and screams as they ran frenetically from one end of the street to another looking for him. His unexpected protector looked at him.

- You are naked —he said, laughing -that's cute.

He was pathetic in his nakedness, with his frozen body trembling, his eyes open, so open that he believed he would never again be able to close them, with his eardrums hurting, with his hands numb and every part of his body trembling, seized by terror.

His protector went over to the dog-house and brought a small blanket.

- Tenne –he said -I am going to fetch you clothing, and something to drink. Hide there.

Wrapped in the blanket, with the pain of his eardrums mounting and his footwear as his only clothing, trembling, he recurred to prayer. He was far away from his beloved Caribbean, trapped in the freezing winter of La Rochelle, close to dying and it was his mother's fault, because it was she who wanted education for her son. It was she who said that he should acquire the characteristic refinement of the European. That is what she said.

- The idea is to demonstrate to your father that, given the proper chance and the corresponding education, you could acquire such brilliance that would surpass your White brother, the legitimate son of your father, that TB stricken, soft, silly boy who in time will put shame on the family.

Those were his mother's words.

Now, the boy returned with a cup full of tea. As he sipped life back into his body, he could still hear the voices; desperate cries they were, since the boys could not explain the sudden disappearance of their prey. And if it were not for the clothes they had managed to tear off his body, they would have thought that they had encountered the devil.

His host went away again, this time to fetch clothes "because you cannot run around naked or you are you going to die." But as he went into the Big House, he left the door open, and out came this huge dog, barking furiously and heading directly toward the intruder.

The Caribbean boy ran for his life, making his way back into the street. He fled, and the boys said "there he is, he will not get away this time." The dog came running after him, as he

*fled towards the dim light that he saw at the end of the street.
Towards the end of the street, there was a different light, and
he knew that there was no other way out, because the dog and
the boys were comingfaster. He ran towards the light, feeling the
blood warming up his cheek, and went out into the small plaza,
full of people. He stopped abruptly in the middle of the plaza,
panicking because of his nakedness, lifting his face to read the
strange street signs.*

To his left, the Pharmacie Rochelaise offered a promotion
of fine perfumes. To his right, on the corner of le Rue St.
Sauveur, the Hotel Henri IV, it's shining facade mocking
time. He closed his eyes, with the perspiration running from
his face, and when he dared to open them again he looked
directly in front into a picturesque collection of photographs
announcing the United Colors of Benito. Out of nowhere a
voice asked kindly.

- Monsieur, is something wrong with you? Are you OK?

He did not answer. He just continued to walk. He passed
the corner of Heyrand, and went out to the square, where
the workers of the CGT were picketing over some Charante
Maritine problem. The square was full of people with banners
and over the loud speaker their leaders harangued them.

- Monsieur –a new voice said –you are going to lose your
camera.

He looked at his white shirt shining immaculately in
the sun. His Bermuda shorts, all too fitting with his slacks
from Sack's Fifth Avenue, New York. His telescopic lens
camera from Japan. His lovely sweater, also form Sack's Fifth
Avenue.

The water behind him; above, the sunbeams and below
the stones that have been there from time immemorial. He
advanced, with his telescopic lens camera hanging from
his neck and with the growing conviction that he knew the
city, step by step. He entered a narrow street, with the total

awareness that if he opened the gate that was halfway down the street –and he did –there would be a garden –and there was –a breath-taking sight. He lifted his camera and took several shots, so he would remember.

A MESSAGE FROM ROSA

As they gathered under the shadow of the blooming tree, I could see on their faces a million Yayah smiles.

THE strange look on Aba's face had gradually given way over the past weeks. She wanted to rest. She had said so once, and although I had convinced her to let me use a month to find out about them, it was very clear to me that there was a strong resolution in her attitude that was not to be changed. At any rate, the truth is that we have been around for a very long time.

She had been seen standing at the window several times over the last week or so. All of us at home had been commenting on this new mania. She just stood there at the window, murmuring strange things about the tree and Timbuktu.

- The tree –she said –should have flourished, but it never did. Our last great-great granddaughter, Aba Nzinga, who had devoted her entire life keeping our home in the best possible condition, sat down to have breakfast.

We sat by her side, watching her have fish soup and a slice of breadfruit. This we did not have in the old days, but by now we consider ours. As Nzinga ate what I guessed could be our last meal together –the month was over –I looked at Aba and smiled. Honestly, I had done all that I could to solve the mystery, but my efforts were all in vain. How could sixteen members of our family just disappear forever? I had had long sessions with an old Oxford professor of history that lived among us. But it was like tracing the origins and whereabouts of nobody, he said, because the files were not reliable.

Aba caught me smiling at her and smiled back. Aba Nzinga also smiled. That might be the last Yayah smile, I taught; the end of the story. Because, it is true, the tree never flourished. Her father's premonition —that blooming would signal better times, while serving as fuel to survival, had had no other practical consequence.

There was no plenitude in our lives. The supreme dignity of the Samamfo was gone.

All we wanted to know was whether or not the Ancestral Spirit of our clans had survived, creating new life in our Nation. It would have been nice to find out if they had kept our Spirit alive, building their homes as we did, living as living people should, without a mask to disguise emptiness.

The son was shining that morning as never before. It was as if the entire world would celebrate the end of this defiance of natural laws.

So it was the end, the ironic finale of the Yayah illusion. All these years of vigil were over. But yet, I did not feel the sting of twenty bees. I knew that the whole memory of the Yayah was here, right here in our room, Aba and myself, and our devoted but now childless descendant.

It was then that we heard someone knocking on the door. A few seconds later, a little girl came running into the living room, asking for Aba.

- Are you Mama Aba? —she asked our great-granddaughter.
- Well...hmm. Aba Nzinga —she said —and...and who are you?
- Miss Rosa asked me to tell Mama Aba that she will never again sit at the back of the bus.
- Who asked you to tell who?
- Miss Rosa, to tell Mama Aba.

Aba Nzinga stood for a moment, with a look on her face that was at the same time astonishment and incredulity.

A message from someone named Rosa to someone who she could not have known.

- And how did you get here? I mean, to our town.
- We came by bus.
- We?
- Yes all of us.
- All of you? Who you?
- We came with the African Diaspora League.
- The African Diaspora League.

Aba and I looked at each other. Her face seemed familiar to us, but before we could react or assimilate the message, another child came into our home, this time unannounced.

Aba stood up, trembling. The boy's face was an exact replica of her father's.

- You *is* Mama Aba? –he asked Aba Nzinga.
- Well, uh…
- Me glad to see you. Well mek a tell you. Rosa will neva neva agen sit a the back a the bus. She done wid the back a the bus.

Aba stumbled to the window and braced herself against the wall while holding on to the window frame. Another child came through the door.

- Mama Aba –he said, adding something about Garífuna people from Central America, and spoke in a language that we could not quiet understand.

"Ounahatu Rosa dimurei, luwagu mañurudügarula anagugiou tidan ugunei" or something of the sort.

We were absolutely amazed and did not know what to do. More and more children came into the house.

"Rosa dire qui elle n'assez pas au derrière au bus."

"Rosa disse que jamais vai sentar na parte de trás do ömnibus".

"Roza tubizi: me lya mpanda mu manga dwe kwendila mu maxitombo ku mbusa."

And, in the midst of the linguistic bombardment we heard Aba Nzinga shouting. It was an ancestral bellow, shaking the earth and imposing immediate silence.

- It's the tree –she said, Mama Aba's tree bloomed. It bloomed!

Aba was smiling and crying, both at the same time.

- Kwame –she said, we should pour a little liquor at the root. With great effort but renewed affection, Aba Nzinga went out to fulfill what resulted to be Mama Aba's last wish, surrounded by smiling and giggling children. As they gathered under the shadow of the blooming tree, I could see on their faces a million Yayah smiles.

Luanda, Angola 1997-Lafayette, Indiana, 2004.

GLOSSARY

Aba: Thursday. One of the names given to each Akan child refers to the day they were born.

Amachi: An Ibo name, meaning "the unpredictable."

Amis des Noirs: Sympathizers of the Black cause in revolutionary France.

Anansi the Spider: An expression of God, who on becoming a trickster lost grace. Popular figure of West African and Caribbean oral traditions.

Before I be a slave: Line of a Gospel song.

Black Shot: Jamaican soldiers in the service of the British.

Bozal: (Bozales) Slave coming directly from Africa. Not baptized.

Brong: (Brongs) A Nation of Ghana. Spanish documentation states that Yangá was from the "Brams".

Bukunu: Kneel down.

Buria and Nigua: Historical sites of Colombian Maroons.

Cottawood: Another sector of Jamaican rebels.

Cowrie shells: used as coins in some parts of Ancient West Africa.

Cat: A medieval instrument of torture.

Cudjoe: Jamaican Maroon freedom fighter.

Cumba: A party.

Cumbes and maniles: Communal ranches. Village household of the Maroons in Latin America.

Efua: Name for a woman born on Friday.

Enslaved: The Africans were not born slaves, but were captured and enslaved.

Except God: (Gye Nyame): An expression from Akan. "No one was around when everything started and no one will live to see the end of everything. Except God!

Fulahghi: An invented name for an African nomadic tribe.

Griot: Poet, depositor of the collective memory.

Gye Nyame: Except God.

It is darkest before dawn: And old traditional saying, used by Costa Rican poet Isaac Felipe Azofeifa.

Jam: From Wolof. Meaning "to party."

Juan de Valladolid: was a Black Spaniard who was appointed around the time of the "discovery" of America to take care of the affairs of the Black population in an area of the country.

Kerapa: Good luck, prosperity. May all be well.

King Bencos: Colombia, 1603.

Kojo and Ekua: Ashanti names.

Kra: A person's unique life-force or Breath of God, given before birth.

Kwaku Esinam New Life: Adapted Ashanti names. Gold Baby, Born on Wednesday, God Heard Me and Gave New Life.

Kwame: Saturday.

La Española: (now Dominican Republic and Haiti) 1522.

Land of the Springs: Meaning of "Jamaica" in the native tongue.

Mali: Ancient African Kingdom. Maintained active commerce with Western Europe.

Mandingo: Person from the Mandinga Nation of Africa.

Man-of-war: Armored ship.

Maroons: Runaway slaves who established autonomous territories from which they resisted re-enslavement and colonization.

Miskito: Afro-Indigenous. African-Native Central American nation, on the coast of Nicaragua. Allies of the British, they sometimes took part in the war against Maroons in Jamaica.

Mogya: Blood. Matrilineal heritage.

Nat Turner: Born in the State of Virginia, USA. His grandmother and mother were enslaved Africans with a great hatred for slavery. Nat led an uprising in 1831. The revolt ended with his execution.

Ni ku tú: Sound from a drum in drum-coded language.

Ntoro: Family heritage, seminal root of the father. Male principle of her father; father's heritage.

Nyaga: Ashanti name, meaning Life is Precious.

Nyame: God as Supreme Being.

Nyamka: Name. Short for Nanyamka. Ashanti, meaning God's gift.

Odomankoma: God as the Infinite.

Orishas: The Ancestors, according to Yoruba tradition.

Saint Iago: Ancient English word for "Santiago". Saint James.

Salto pa'tra: In the caste system, if someone married a person oflower caste, he was considered doing a "salto para atrás" meaning a backward leap.

Samamfo: The common lore of the people, including the ancestors, the living and the unborn, their culture, their traditions. According to an Ashanti saying, a person is never really dead. Samanfo: Sprit and lore of the ancestors, the community and the traditions that give us our identity, the cradle of the ones to come. For in reality, no one is actually dead.

Scataration: Caribbean English for Diaspora.

Shangó: The Yoruba god of war, lightening and thunder.

Songhai: An Ancient African Tributary State.

Spaniards coming back: Jamaica had been formerly under Spanish rule.

Sumsum: Soul of a person or of a people. Soul of the group, communal soul.

Tercerones: One of the many categories of the Hispanic caste system

Tete Abosom: Minor communal deities, children of God. Somewhat similar to Guardian Angels.

The Code: Reference to "Las Siete Partidas" Ancient Spanish Slave Code

Timbuktu and Djenne: two cultural and political centers in Ancient West African tributary states.

Tree of forgetfulness: A ceremony enforced by some slave traders to sort of "brain wash" the Africans. The idea was to break off all psychological ties with their people.

Wahkey: From Wolof. Meaning "its cool, no problem." Creole: White French Caribbean.

Yaa: (Asase Yaa) Deity of the Akan, God's Feminine Persona, in care of the Earth and of Social Morality.

Yangá: A Mexican Black hero, who led a successful uprising against Spanish slavery at the beginning of the XVII century.

Yayah: An invented name for an African nation.

Zamba: Afro-Native American mestizo.

Other books in English by Quince Duncan

The Best Short Stories of Quince Duncan (1996) Translated by Dellita Martin-Ogunsula. San José: Editorial Costa Rica.

A Message from Rosa (2007). Bilingual English-Spanish edition. San José: EUNED.

CPSIA information can be obtained
at www.ICGtesting.com
Printed in the USA
FSOW01n2326211216
28762FS